HOW TO

FALL

FOR A

COWBOY

BY

CASSANDRA JOELLE

For the reader curled up with a pumpkin muffin and a mug of cider- may these pages bring you laughter, cozy fall sweetness, and a gentle reminder that God's love is the richest feast of all.

Author's Note

This story touches on body image, self-worth, over-exercising and restrictive eating, but always through the lens of hope, humor, and God's truth that we are wonderfully made.

THE ROUNDUP

CHAPTER 1:

BLESS THIS HOT MESS

There's a reason that mankind seemed to "couple-up" during the 'ber months. It wasn't scientific and needed to be studied, but there was something about trading your spaghetti strap tanks for henleys that made you want to be the big spoon. In Maple Haven, Wyoming, an idyllic place full of a flaming grove of maple and aspen trees nestled in the Rocky Mountains, autumn vibes were on steroids, which didn't make it any easier to fight the desires of repealing my singledom. That season was what everyone looked forward to for our incredible, awe-inspiring fall foliage. Plus, we had tourists who would drive hundreds of miles away to leaf-peep beautiful valleys and hillsides, filling up our town with a bustling economy. So, it was capitalized on, and we did it well.

With every restaurant having their own pumpkin, cinnamon, or pecan flavored special, I can now tell you what pumpkin enchiladas taste like. Clothing stores stocked the coziest sweaters and socks, of which I owned more pairs than we had days of the year when I could wear them. My weakness was the chunky knit scarves that would scratch at your neck with their wooly material, giving "redneck" from the irritation. Of course, there was no shortage of cute western boots of every variety and color in our Wyoming town. We knew how to do "cowboy" there, and we did it well. And at my nail salon, *The Cozy Cuticle,* we offered a selection of fall-infused treatments.

Our most popular foot spa was the Pumpkin Spice Pedi. Sure, it was nothing more than a spa pedicure with a heavenly scented cinnamon and pumpkin soak for your feet and extra-cute fall decals for your toes. But the main event was our multi-day festival centered around all things rodeo, pageantry, and pies: the *Pumpkin Stampede* was the pinnacle of Maple Haven's existence.

The *Pumpkin Stampede,* happening annually in the first week of October, was what we were known for. Other holidays practically didn't exist in our little cozy autumn corner of Wyoming. The festival would start with a parade, the succession of which would close down our entire town. It was led by the town's Pumpkin Queen, voted in the year prior. The rodeo would have bronc and bull riders from all over Wyoming, Montana, and Idaho compete, along with a barrel racing event. The winners of such would be named Maple Haven's Rodeo King & Queen, along with a hefty cash prize and a custom gold-plated belt buckle.

The festival involved a blue ribbon and respect-earning pie bake off, judged by a panel of previous winners of the title. Though we allowed competitors from out of state to come for our rodeo, the pie bake-off rules contested that competitors must live right there in Maple Haven, Wyoming. It made for some goofy instances of people trying to hole up in a hotel for a week before to claim residency, so the rules were enforced strictly.

Then, there was the cowboy bachelor auction, which was arguably the most attended event. Women came from all over to bid on the men, and men attended to tease their friends on the display stage. It was always a wild, fun event, and the proceeds went to amazing local causes. One year, our town earned enough to re-roof the animal shelter. Next, we were able to fix damage to the local baseball field caused by a storm and an irrigation pump at the town's golf course. Recreation for our small community proved to be very important in the off-seasons— basically anything that wasn't autumn.

The Pumpkin Stampede festivities ended with a hoedown. Usually held in the county's largest riding arena that had straw bales for sitting and twinkling lights for romancing, it was always the worst part for me since I'd never managed to have a date. But that year, that would be changing.

As it turned out, I was ready for more. My friends were paired off to their forever guys, and I remained the lone wolf. When Laney and Blair wanted to go out? I got to be the perpetual fifth-wheel to their dates. And I didn't think anyone *aspired* to be a fifth wheel. My goal for that fall was to change all of that. I was ready to hone in on a guy of my own.

My goal for that very autumn season? Securing a man of my own. My heart said it should be a rugged, manly man whose masculinity complimented my femininity.

And as it turned out, I had one in mind. The only problem? He had yet to acknowledge that we would be perfect together, or, in any sense at all. But I had a plan. All I needed to do was become the type of girl whom that particular gym-lover would want: a spunky, fit, gym babe. What could possibly go wrong?

Sighing, I pulled out a bag of fall decor and took it outside of the nail salon. The official start date of the autumn season was late September, but in Maple Haven, it was the day after Labor Day. Since we were at the end of September, with the Stampede the following week, Autumn was in full swing. As I decorated the outside of the salon, while Laney and Blair, the sisters who co-owned the salon with me, were decorating the inside window displays with glittery decals and faux pumpkins in colors never found in nature, I felt the faintest chill in the air. A warm scent of apple crossed my senses. My feet were sweating in my Ugg boots. I might have jumped the gun wearing those, when that week was still arguably sandal weather. But all of that was changing—the next day, the weather would finally be dropping. Summer, as we knew it, was finally over. Though autumn was short-lived and often came late in Maple Haven, it was the best season, and all the residents there savored it for its beauty and fun.

"Ginger! Do you have time for a fill?"

I looked down awkwardly from my step ladder as I attempted to hang a colorful glitter leaf garland, complete with miniature acorns hot glued to the rope on the nail salon's pink awning. Standing below me in anticipation was the gorgeous blonde Lexie Van Arden; former rodeo queen and the closest thing to a socialite in Maple Haven.

"Sure thing, Lexie. Why don't you go pick out a color, and I'll be right there."

"You are a lifesaver! I broke two nails this week and I'm seeing Mark tomorrow. Can't let him think I'm a werewolf or something." She hurried inside, smiling.

Lexie was a regular, and I knew what she considered a broken nail, others would consider a scuff.

"Want me to take over, Ginger?" Laney poked her slinky blonde head out the salon door as a large gust of wind swept through, bringing the faintest batch of sun-dried leaves along with it, tickling ankles as they flew by.

"Yes, please! Thank you." I stepped down, nearly missing the step and accidentally using the end of the garland I was still holding to keep me upright. The whole strip of fake leaves and plastic acorns came down in one fell swoop.

"Yikes. Here, girl. Come down from there before we have to file a workman's comp claim." I stepped down from the ladder, Laney holding back her laughter at the mishap. Nearby, a generator from a food truck kicked on, killing the peaceful ambiance.

"I'm a walking insurance claim lately. I don't remember ever being this clumsy? Thank you, Laney. Maybe Bruce can come hang this?" Laney's husband Bruce was a local handyman, and he never passed up a chance to come see his wife in action.

"You read my mind." She wound up the garland like a garden hose around her toned arm and pulled out her cell phone. I stepped into the salon, greeting Lexie, who wore a near-perfect set of acrylic nails that I had only done a week ago.

Smiling, I pulled out my file and asked her about her upcoming date with Mark, the man she had been seeing for six months.

"He's taking me to see the Phantom of the Opera tomorrow. Can you believe it? The man I thought had no culture outside of this rodeo town whatsoever."

"Mark? The man who wears a white *Stetson* with sandals and *cargo pants?*" Blair chimed in as she put in a vanilla amber diffuser in the wall sconce.

"I can't believe it either, ladies. I'm telling you, I've cracked the code: It is possible to change a man after all."

"Well, he's not really *changed* though, is he? Does he still buy all of his clothing from wholesale stores ?" Laney chimed in.

Lexie shrugged. "Mark loves a bargain."

"Do you see a future with Mark?" I asked, while trading in my file for the nail drill.

"Oh yes. Definitely. Mark is husband material. He adores me; it's mutual, though. I love how he looks at me like I'm the last piece of pecan pie at Thanksgiving."

"Okay... But if I see you in sweats that can only be bought in bulk, I'll take that as a signal you've developed Stockholm Syndrome, and you need to be rescued," Laney quipped.

"You *are* a little more fashionable than Mark, Lexie." I quietly mentioned it to her, as when I looked at the two of them, I would've never in a million years paired them up. Lexie was a former barrel racer, and she was the three-time winner of the Pumpkin Queen pageant there in Maple Haven, starting in her sophomore year of high school. Had she not gone out of state for college on a full rodeo scholarship in Montana, she probably would've kept winning the title. She was known for her oversized turquoise jewelry, platinum hair, and year-round tan, thanks to a tanning bed in her basement. Her clothing included gorgeous, luxurious brands like *Pendleton*, *Old Gringo*, and *MissMe*.

"I know Mark doesn't seem like all that, Ginger. But his soul speaks the language of my own in ways no one else could. There's more to love than what's on the surface. Yes, he's a cheap curmudgeon who has no fashion sense or taste. But what he does love is me. He wants to make me happy. When my first husband died in that horse accident, I thought I'd never find anyone else.

When I met Mark, I still thought that. I wouldn't go out with him. His persistence eventually softened my heart. Now, six months into our courtship and I'm having the time of my life." Lexie speaking of her love made me yearn for a story of my own.

"I'm so happy for you, Lexie," I said, while Blair and Laney chimed in identical platitudes.

"What about you, Ginger? Any luck with love lately?" Lexie asked. I shrugged.

"No, not really. I just want a *real* man. I like guys that are strong," I huffed.

"I don't blame you one bit. You need a *manly* man, Ginger. A protector. A shield for the outside world." Lexie went on. As she described the type of man she thought I needed, I agreed- it all sounded pretty nice. I did want a man like that. In fact, I think I knew just where to look for one.

"There are some cute ones at the gym..." I trailed off.

"Yes, muscle men! Now, there we go! What next?" Lexie pressed, while Laney and Blair knowingly smiled.

"Ginger, you could have anyone you wanted. You just need to pray that God sends you the right man and trust in his timing."

"Thanks, Blair. I totally agree with that. God is very much in control of my love life." I was filing away when another thought came to me that I felt I should just go ahead and blurt out.

"Well, there is someone in particular that I find very attractive..." Lexie readjusted in her seat and put her opposite hand under her chin.

"Do tell! Who is it?" She looked at me eagerly.

"His name is Dallas—" Lexie cut me off.

"Dallas down at the Maple Muscle gym?" she blurted out.

"Yes, that's him. Do you know him?" Lexie shook her head.

"Some of my fellow rodeo queens do their fitness training there with him. I've heard he's a pretty good trainer. And pretty cute, too." She winked. I felt a twinge of jealousy hearing that the most beautiful women in our town were spending time with the guy I'm crushing on, but I prayed for my feelings, and they passed.

"Agreed. Dallas is *fine*," I smiled.

"You mean 'The Protein Poet'." Laney could barely control her laughter as they spoke of my future husband.

"Yes, I know he's a bit of a gym bro," I smirked, not letting their teasing penetrate my feelings for Dallas. He was a beautiful man; tall, tousled blonde hair, and his body wasn't just muscular; it was *ripped to shreds.* He always looked like he just walked off a photo shoot. Or a protein bar commercial. He was part-owner in the gym, too.

"A bit? The man speaks in motivational riddles. I asked him once if he could tell me how to change the weight setting on the leg press and he said, 'You miss all the lunges you don't take.' What does that even *mean*, Ginger?" Laney looked at me with a hysteric expression. The other ladies were giggling.

"He's aspirational. A still water that runs deep, if you will. Besides, he has other interests. I think he's training for a triathlon," I said.

"The only thing deep about that guy is his love for the mirror," Blair added.

"Okay, okay. Well, don't worry, ladies. He still doesn't know I exist, so he won't be my boyfriend anytime soon. That is at least..." I trailed off.

"What? Are you going to roll up in there and hire him as a foot model for our Instagram account?" Laney asked. As much as it hurt to admit, the man I'd been pining away for the last year, since I joined the gym, still had yet to strike up a full-blown conversation with me. But that was about to change soon. I had a plan, after all.

"No, I've never seen his feet, so I can't say they would be good on our Instagram. I had a better idea. I just signed up for some one-on-one personal training lessons with him."

"Good for you, Ginger. Go after what you want." Lexie applauded my decision.

"No comment from the peanut gallery?" My eyebrows raised in the direction of Laney and Blair, who had an opinion on everything, but were bizarrely quiet on that plan of mine.

"No, I have none. Do you, Blair, have anything you'd like to say?" Laney looked to her sister.

"Nothing." Blair finished up the window display that looked gorgeous with the matte pink walls of the salon that were covered in crown molding, while I took out a brush and started applying fresh acrylic.

"Okay, then," I smiled with satisfaction.

"Just do me one favor." Laney stepped towards the door, as I saw her husband Bruce had arrived to hang up the garland. "When you see him, say 'hashtag workout.' I want to know if his brain functions on a secret AI robotic code or not."

"Ha-ha, very funny," I smirked at her. Though they gave me lots of hassle on my love interest, Laney and Blair were my best friends in the world. They were two years apart, and I was in the middle. Growing up in a small town could either mean friends for life or making a recluse out of people. I was thankful every day for the opportunity God had given me to spend time with those wonderful ladies.

"Ginger, please be careful. I don't want to see you getting hurt, physically *or* emotionally. Okay?" Blair pleaded with me. I nodded in reply, not looking to her to make eye contact.

Topping off Lexie's acrylics, she selected a beautiful teal gel polish that accentuated her turquoise jewelry. As I finished up her fresh set, Blair jumped up like *The Pumpkin Perk Cafe* coffee shop had just released a new twist on her favorite spiced chai latte. "Oh my!"

"What is it, Blair?" I called out, putting the last of the top coat on Lexie's nails. Blair ran outside and out of sight. When the door was open, a gentle hum could be heard nearby.

"I bet it's that dessert truck we've been hearing about for weeks. Mark is on the city council and a man, actually; he's about your age," she winked, "and applied for a special permit to serve autumn delectables all season long. A real entrepreneur spirit, if you ask me," Lexie smiled.

"Sounds like my downfall. All this time I've been spending at the gym, and a dessert truck gets parked nearby? I better just stay away. That's a slippery slope." Ever since I saw Dallas at the gym, I'd been returning regularly to see if anything might happen between us. A look. A gaze. Heck, at that point, I'd been pining away for him so hard that I would have taken a tap on the shoulder to ask if I was still using the *Butt Blaster 3000* machine as a means to strike up a conversation. I hadn't had much luck, but my physique was really showing the difference. I was looking shapely, but trim. I'd been following a structured diet of proteins and greens all year long, and it was getting increasingly blander by the date. I knew if I gave that food truck one look, it would be bad news for my waistline.

Lexie laughed. "I get it. But I am of the mindset that pumpkin pie, when it's made with pure pumpkin puree, is good for you." She gave me a dazzling smile as she took her hands out of the UV lamp, gave me cash for the service, and left. When she exited, Blair came in holding a pink paper cup with a pumpkin printed on the beige paper koozie.

"Ginger—look at this! Have you ever seen anything more Instagram worthy in your life? Besides our salon, I mean. And the taste is heavenly!" She was right. The truck definitely knew who his customers were: fall-loving, coffee-drinking *women*.

"Oh, gosh. That's cute, alright. What is it?" It smelled decadent and creamy, rich with spices.

"It's a pumpkin spice chai with maple foam and a splash of Madagascar vanilla syrup." She took a long gulp. "I've never had a better drink. I mean it."

Favorite Fall Recipes (coffee edition)
One part pumpkin syrup
Espresso to taste, while you play with its pronunciation
(must roll R's to gain full effect)
Three parts full-fat milk
3 handfuls of candy corn to snack on while you figure out the milk steamer
After 90 minutes of troubleshooting, find nearest coffee shop

"Better than *The Pumpkin Perk Café*'s chai that you told me you want poured on your gravesite one day? I don't believe it." Blair had a flair for the dramatics, but she held her ground.

"Believe it, Ginger. This takes the lead for frothy drinks in my life. Maybe you should go out there and see it for yourself?" She looked at me with a devious smile.

"See what? My workout goals go down the drain?" I put my hands on my hips.

"Don't tell me you want to lose more weight? Ginger—you are the most beautiful woman in Maple Haven, inside and out. Women would rob a pumpkin spice factory for your stunning, flaming hair that matches your namesake. Your hazel eyes with gold flecks that reflect the autumn light. You are a literal walking Pinterest board for autumn vibes. Don't let anyone tell you differently, and for all things good in the world, get yourself something from that truck."

"Thank you for the pep talk, Blair. I don't really have a goal in mind, I just..." I didn't want to say it out loud.

"You just want to become what kind of woman you think Dallas wants?" She always could read me like a book.

"Maybe," I shrugged. I hated feeling vulnerable, but she was right about that.

"Look—working out? Very healthy. I'm happy for you. Eating healthy, that's wonderful. But you can't tell me you're going to suffer all the way through the pumpkin-everything season without sampling anything, can you? Besides, you don't know what Dallas wants because you've never said a word to each other." Before I could answer, Laney burst through the door. A gust of wind howling behind her.

"This wind! It's happening, ladies—fall is near!" With the gust of wind brought a tantalizing fragrance of sweet treats.

Mouth- watering baked apple, rich pumpkin, and buttery pecan fragrances all in one. "Can I get that scent in a candle already?" Laney asked rhetorically.

"Do you want to see if we can change our diffuser scent, sis?" Blair asked.

"Nah, we better not go too overboard, since those Pumpkin Spice Pedicures can be sickeningly sweet after a long day of them." We all laughed and agreed. By the end of that season, we were usually ready for a break. As I looked out the front window, dolled up to the nines with autumn decor, I prayed to God that with the wind, He would bring something new to my life.

CHAPTER 2:
HAY THERE, HANDSOME

The next morning started with a trip to *The Pumpkin Perk Cafe*. Just because there was a new food truck in town that was also serving drinks, didn't mean I should've turned my back on the business that I'd been frequenting since I was a high school student. Sure, their espresso machine sometimes acted like it was haunted, shooting out chards of coffee beans into their drinks. They also didn't often have fresh baked goods and their service was lackluster. But the owners, Kevin and Charla, had been trying to sell the shop all year to chase a new dream of existing only in warm weather. In the real estate listing, the first line read, "Florida is calling our names." I didn't blame them one bit; I just wished in the meantime they could get refills of my favorite coffee syrups. After reading the list of what they did have in stock, I settled on a combination that sounded good.

Ray, the barista who was the definition of indifferent, waltzed over and sighed. "What'll it be, Ginger?"

Gee, had I interrupted something there?

"I'll take three sugar-free Marshmallow Maple Lattes to go."

"We're out of the carrying trays." He stared at me blankly.

"Fine. I'm just going to the salon." He nodded and rang me up, flipping the tablet screen around so I could select his tip. I raised my eyebrows as the suggested amount started at 25%. "Any luck on the sale?" I asked while he made my drinks at a glacial pace.

"Not yet. They've had some people come by to look, of course. But nobody with any business sense."

I smirked.

Leaving the cafe, I held a cup in each hand, with the third in between. As long as I walked slowly, it would be fine. With only steps left to get there, something caught my western bootie, and it wasn't only my drinks that went flying. I found myself lying face down on the sidewalk, my arm having been my saving grace to my fall as my head landed on it. People rushed over while the hot liquid of my expensive drinks was pooling around my hair, drenching my ends in it.

"What in the world? What happened, Ginger?" Laney ran out of the salon to see if I was alright. An older couple helped me to my feet as I looked for what I tripped on. All of the usual suspects were present; scattered pumpkins, hay bales and scarecrows were everywhere, but nothing I hadn't walked past a hundred times that month.

"I'll be okay. I don't think I'm hurt, other than my feelings, that is. Those coffees were expensive as all get out." I traced back a few steps and saw a bright orange extension cord snaking over the sidewalk. I picked up the cord and followed it until I saw the culprit: a cheerful, pumpkin-themed food truck. The extension cord? It was being used to power a strand of twinkle lights which were currently being hung up for a broad shouldered, curly haired man in flannel with a cowboy hat. The sheer *audacity* of that man!

"That's okay, Ginger. I'll get us some coffees from Tucker." Laney picked up the cups I had thrown in my fall and put them in a sidewalk garbage can. I followed her with my eyes as she walked right up to the man that caused my fall and greeted him with a warm smile. She must have been telling him what happened because he sharply turned my direction, but I quickly looked away, ducking into the salon. There was something about that guy that really crunched my leaves, and I didn't know why.

As I was studying my appointment book and wringing the last of the lattes out of my hair, Laney pranced in and placed another one of those adorable pink cups on my station, with a sinfully fragrant muffin. "It's an apple fritter *muffin,* Ginger. Don't tell me you can resist." She tapped her foot and smirked at me.

"Watch me." My mouth was watering on overdrive at the sweet, sugary scent. As I peeked out of the corner of my eye, I swore I saw candied pecans mixed in.

"What if I told you it was made by a *cowboy?"* She tapped her foot waiting for my reply that never came. The man that made me fall, and who was taunting me with his intoxicating scented desserts, did not warrant my reaction. "Fine, suit yourself. I will enjoy Tucker's peace offering. He is very sorry to cause your fall—he's removed the cord. I let him plug into our building. Since we are at the end of the cul-de-sac, no one will trip. Problem solved." She kept talking while I started to tune her out. "I also waived your right to sue him."

"Mhmm. Sounds good. What kind of coffee is it?" But when I looked up, Laney couldn't hear me. It looked like she was doing a ballroom dance with the muffin as she nibbled at her partner.

"This is the best thing I've ever eaten in my life. This is better than that wedding cake I paid three thousand dollars for!"

Did I mention that both Blair *and* Laney had a flair for the dramatic? And Laney, being newly wed to Bruce, was still excitedly talking about her nuptials. That whole situation with the sweets being shoved down my throat just felt...strange. Different. Out of my comfort zone. I surely wasn't ready to jump on the bandwagon and kiss my diet goodbye.

The delightful chime of our door rang, breaking Laney out of her trance *dance,* and our first customers of the day started arriving for their appointments. As Laney, Blair and I seated our clients in the pedicure chairs, a familiar scent filled the room.

"Pumpkin spice pedicure time, ladies," Blair announced, smiling as she enjoyed the sweet, sugary scent. Since the customers all knew each other, as everyone in Maple Haven did, Laney snapped a cute picture for our salon's Instagram account.

"Hashtag *cute!*"

As I chatted with my client about what shade of mulberry wine polish would suit her best, she took a sip of a coffee I hadn't noticed her walk in with. In a distinctively *pink* cup. Then I saw it: Everyone in the salon, except me, was drinking one of this guy's coffees. And seemingly enjoying the heck out of it, too. As my coffee went warm behind me, I felt myself starting to stew on the fact that it felt personal. The guy was there to damper my diet. I'd successfully avoided all carbs and *fun* since January... And pumpkin pie was my *favorite.* I would not give in. I said a silent prayer for strength, as the sweet scent of the delightful treats seemed to get stronger.

"That's it. I'm convinced—it's a cult," I said as our freshly pampered clients walked out the door together, carefully tapping their pretty, polished feet in their flip flops as they waddled back over to the pumpkin themed truck.

"Isn't everything pumpkin spice flavored a bit of a cult, Ginger? Come on, just take a sip. It's sugar free, Ginger. No guilt." Laney held up the lukewarm coffee still sitting where she placed it. I looked out the salon window to see our customers leaving with little pink paper bags stamped with bright maple leaves but not giving the man another glance. Sighing, I took the cup from Laney's hand.

"Fine. But I can't imagine this is any better than the lattes I picked up for us this morning. I had a sip of it before I spilled it, and it was *very good*."

Laney smirked, while Blair excused herself to get a refill of her own. I put the cup to my lips and took the tiniest sip.

At first, I was surprised at the heat it had retained while I neglected it all morning. Then, there was a delightful spice to the coffee that perfectly blended with a creaminess from the oat milk, a strong hint of vanilla, a kick of marshmallow, and the strength of a rich, strong brew of hazelnut espresso behind it. The coffee was a dream. I was beside myself, as my sip turned into a full-blown *chug*.

Laney stood with her arms crossed and eyebrow cocked. "Well? Would you like me to take you to the cult leader? He's actually really nice. An ex-bronc rider, *apparently*. It doesn't get any more *masculine* than that, wouldn't you say, Ginger?" My mind went from pleasantly surprised to annoyed. Laney's favorite sport was to use my words against me for my own reminder. Blair came back holding two cups of coffee, handing one to Laney.

"Tucker thought you might need another," she smirked.

"Why thank you, Tucker. Hear that, Ginger? He's so good at anticipating needs."

I rolled my eyes and noticed Laney and Blair both giving me a stare-down.

"A-ha! Is this what the agenda is here? You guys want me to meet Tucker to get my mind off of Dallas? I know you don't like Dallas, but you haven't even given him a chance."

"Ginger, Dallas hasn't even given *you* a chance," Blair said abruptly. The look on her face that followed showed remorse, but the words stung. "Look, I'm sorry, Ginger. You just don't see how beautiful you are. How beautiful that you've always been. It's a crime that Dallas hasn't noticed you. But maybe it's time to meet other men who wouldn't make that same mistake? And you just said you wanted to meet someone *new*."

My mind wrestled with the conversation. I was not ready to believe that Dallas wasn't into me because he didn't know me yet.

"He just seems like a really good guy. He's a cowboy *and* a baker? Yes, please! Plus, when was the last time we had someone new in town? It's kind of exciting, when you think about it." Laney acted giddy as she downed her second tall latte of the morning. Her phone made a buzzing noise, and she pulled it out of her pink, button-fly jeans and looked down. "Aww. Bruce asked if I want him to bring me a treat from the pumpkin cart."

Bruce doted on Laney, and it was beautiful. They started dating two years ago and the engagement and marriage was quick to follow. Though they grew up knowing of one another, she never considered him in a romantic sense until we bought the salon. Laney had a dream of crown molding on all the walls and when she called a local handyman to do it, in walked Bruce. She said it was love at the millionth site.

"Tucker is really nice, Ginger," Blair chimed in. Laney went to sit in the pedicure massage chair, kicking off her Ugg boots and immersing herself in her texts with her husband.

"So, why don't *you* get to know him?" It was a low blow for me to say that, considering Blair was in the midst of a courtship with a young pastor who was considering a year- long mission overseas. "I'm sorry, Blair. I don't know what's wrong with me today. I woke up on the wrong side of the bed."

Laney looked up from her phone to chime in, as I gave Blair a quick hug. "More like on the wrong side of a pumpkin chai. Just go get one, Ginger." Laney was right. I needed some caffeine, for the sake of my friendships and my job.

"Fine. I'll go. Can I get anyone anything?" I looked around the stations, seeing traces of pink cups everywhere.

"I think we're all set," Blair smiled.

"I'm good. Bruce is bringing me something in a little bit. I better save room. But you should totally get a sample of the goods." Laney took another sip of her coffee and winked at me.

"Very funny. I'll be right back." As my hand clenched the tongue of the golden door handle, I peeked outside. No one was standing at the truck. From that angle, I couldn't see the man inside, either. Opening the door, a cool wind passed by, sending a flurry of golden leaves along with it. My shoes crunched on the crisp, wind-blown leaves as I walked over to the end of our cul-de-sac. The man inside had his back to me and didn't hear me walk up. I used the time to look things over. Looking at the truck head-on was truly a treat for the senses. The truck was a lovely beige color and had a bright white and pink striped awning. Delectable treats were artfully written all over the menu that hung from the counter. The offerings ranged from apple and pecan to pumpkin everything. Seeing it up close, I took back everything I said before; that was exactly the cute addition Maple Haven needed in the fall. I was genuinely impressed that a man came up with all of that cute branding. He must have had a girlfriend or a wife, I decided. That certainly took the pressure off things. I could let it go that Laney and Blair thought I would like him, because the man wasn't available. He couldn't be.

Small Town Wisdom

An expensive coffee never solves your problems. It only gives you the caffeine to make the problems seem worse.

"Hi, there." I croaked, my voice sounding a little rougher since I'd had almost nothing to drink that day, except for the lukewarm coffee that was still delightful. "I'd like a latte, please." The man turned around, and I was met with a smiling face. He had tan skin, light green eyes, and a prominent nose. His hands looked rugged. His hair was curly, in an out-of-control way, but it was cut short and shaved on the sides. There was something about him that felt...kind. I also couldn't help but notice just how good looking he was.

"Hey there, darlin'. I'm Tucker Callahan. You must be Ginger?" He held out a hand as I robotically shook it, feeling a little entranced by his cowboy drawl.

"Yes, how did you know?" I looked back at the salon, thinking they had shown him my photo or something and saw Laney and Blair's faces pressed up against the picture window. They quickly pretended to be fixing the glittery pink and turquoise leaf window decals.

"I heard about your falling, but by the time I got out of my truck here, you were gone. Laney met me to talk about the cord. I'm very sorry about that, by the way. I hope you can forgive me." His eyes laid on my face. He was so... genuine. I liked that.

"Ahh, yeah, I was just testing the laws of gravity." I looked away, embarrassed.

"And what were your results?"

"Still working," I snapped my fingers, and started looking over the coffee menu. Every drink he had listed sounded absolutely divine: from white chocolate gingerbread mochas to brown sugar pecan lattes. My mouth was watering as I skimmed the selections. "I'll take a sugar free..." My voice trailed off as I felt the presence of someone walk up behind me. I peeked over my shoulder to see it was Bruce. His phone started ringing immediately.

"Hi sweetie, I'll be right—" his eyebrows raised, "Oh, of course I'll come look at a project inside the salon first." He put his phone in his pocket and for a moment it looked like he was going to announce his departure before looking at both me and Tucker and tiptoeing away. I smirked at Laney and Blair's attempt to couple me up with this guy. There wasn't anything wrong with him or how he looked; in fact, it was hard not to notice his lovely jawline or the dimple on his right cheek. I'd just been working so hard at getting Dallas. And maybe this guy represented everything I was trying to avoid.

"How about I make you something just for you?" Tucker caught me by surprise.

"Oh—okay," I said hesitantly.

"Great. What is your fondest memory as a child from autumn?" An instant lump formed in the back of my throat.

"My grandma's spiced cider," I said without even thinking. He smiled, revealing a beautiful warmth to his eyes when he did so and nodded. As he started steaming milk, he asked me another question.

"Do you like pumpkin pie?" An innocent loaded question.

"Of course I do. It's my favorite dessert on earth. But I'm sort of in a cut phase right now." Tucker turned around and gave me a confused look.

"What is a cut phase?"

"Oh, it's where you are actively losing to meet a goal weight." Tucker's eyes didn't meet mine again for a moment, and I considered how my words sounded. I knew I was at a good weight, and Laney and Blair often told me lately I was borderline *too* thin. They were concerned I was taking it too far. I was pretty focused on healthy eating, though it was my workouts I may have been taking too far. I'd been at the gym almost six days a week since January, as my interest in Dallas grew with each session. Standing there, swimming in my statement about losing weight, I considered for the first time that the girls were right; instead of trying to honor God with my self-discipline, I was doing it all for Dallas to notice me.

"I respect everyone's choices of whether or not they wish to indulge in a sweet treat. But God created you in his image, and by golly, that includes your taste buds, darlin'." Tucker winked and smiled as he handed me the coveted pink cup. "Here you go; the Ginger special." My senses swirled as I experienced the aromas.

"What is it?" I asked, waiting to take a sip before I heard the flavor combination.

"It's a caramel spiced apple latte with a cinnamon foam. Oh, and it's sugar free." He smiled. My lips couldn't touch the cup fast enough after I heard the description and the flavors were out of this world. Memories of my grandmother's spiced cider flooded my mind, and my heart was warmed by the buttery caramel notes. The foam was the perfect topper, adding a bit of a zest.

"It's...amazing. Thank you, Tucker." I pulled out a five-dollar bill, and he handed me back a dollar. I placed it in his tip jar. "What if I had said my favorite memory was roasted turkey?"

Tucker laughed, revealing a sparkle to his eyes. "I would have used the turkey syrup." He threw his arms up in laughter. "It was a chance I was willing to take that you'd want something sweet. Thank you, Ginger. I hope you come back for some treats or pie soon. I've got samples of all the flavors if you ever want a taste. I've gotta say, baked goods are really my specialty."

I waved and left, drinking almost half the latte just on the short walk back to the salon. Laney and Blair were pretending to show Bruce a light fixture that they wanted changed when I walked back inside.

"Oh hi, Ginger. How are you?" Bruce said with an honest notion to his voice, while Laney and Blair looked at me sheepishly.

"Whatcha got there, Ginger?" Laney pointed to my cup.

"Hi Bruce," I turned my back to them so they couldn't see my expression. "Just some coffee."

"Just *some* coffee? Or did he do that thing where he makes you a cup that is just for you?" All that talk about my drink made me dying to take another swig. I resisted as long as I could, finally downing what was left of the contents in my pink cup.

"Fine!" I stood, unable to hide my newly caffeinated smile. "It's the best coffee I've ever had! Are you happy?" I turned to see Laney, Blair, *and* Bruce looking smug at me. "You too, Bruce? What is it with you guys?"

Both ladies looked to Bruce, who was shuffling his feet. "He just seems like a really nice guy, Ginger. Maybe you *should* get to know him."

"He seems fine, and assuming he would even want to go out with me... But I didn't feel that 'spark' that I do with Dallas." Laney and Blair both rolled their eyes. "Before you come after me, think about all this beautiful pink fall merchandising; there is no way that he doesn't already have a girlfriend. Or maybe even a wife! You guys might be trying to hook me up with a married man. Thou shalt not commit *adultery*, remember?" I crossed my arms and tapped my foot. They weren't the only ones who could be dramatic. Blair gave me an annoyed look.

Laney held up her cup from earlier. "He has better branding than my entire social media platform. And I took *classes* on that. I think this guy is a real genius. Or at least a man who knows how to hire a graphic designer." Laney winked at Bruce, who proudly had his handyman logo designed by a professional and constantly wore his branding every day on a different colored shirt.

I rolled my eyes. "Exactly. A man who is not only comfortable with all of the pink cups and bags, but is leading with this darling, lovely, *Pinterest-worthy* feminine branding? He's secure, that's for sure. Probably in a long-term, loving relationship with a woman who models swimsuits or something. He's got nothing to prove."

"How specific...?" Blair took a couple steps in my direction and leaned in, not speaking any quieter. "Do you have low blood sugar? I know just the guy for that." She pointed to the truck out the window and I threw my hands up in the air when the front door chimed. The four of us turned, all revealing beaming smiles when our next clients walked through the door. Though we were constantly bantering, we were able to shut it off like a light switch when customers were present.

"Hello, Mrs. Peabody. And Mrs. Haverly! So nice to see you ladies." I greeted them and started the foot baths so the water could get to temperature.

Mrs. Haverly, somewhat known as the town's busybody, who was always a plethora of local information, excitedly kicked off her sandals.

Ginger's Polished Thoughts:
Life is busy and fast. Make your nails look like disco balls so that you get distracted, too.

"We would like the pumpkin spice pedicures, with those little glitter decals like last year, please and thank you."

"You got it, ladies. So, what are you up to today? Doing anything fun?" I started chatting with them while I helped Mrs. Peabody into the chair. The ladies were sisters and ten years apart in age, so it seemed like Mrs. Haverly was acting as a caretaker for Mrs. Peabody of late.

Mrs. Haverly took the lead in conversation, as recently, her sister couldn't speak as well. "This is our first stop. We wanted to come earlier, and I know we like to pretend that it's fall here early, but when it's still seventy out, oh, I don't know—I just can't get on board with pumpkin yet. But now it's finally starting to cool. Our feet wait for this heavenly scented treat all summer long." The aroma of the nourishing bubbles was so divine, I wondered just how long I could keep up that diet of mine if I was starting to foam at the mouth for a foot spa.

"And we are so glad to have you. Speaking of pumpkin," Laney winked at me, knowing she could get away with that since we had customers present, "did you see that we have a new food truck outside?"

"You mean that darling boy, Tucker, serving all things *autumn?*"Mrs. Haverly reached into her bucket bag, pulling out a pink paper bag with colorful maple leaves adorning it. "We've already been twice, and golly, I think he's only been set up four hours!"

"And what cute cups and bags, right?" Blair chimed in.

"I know. Apparently the whole idea was his sister's. . ." Mrs. Haverly spoke. I froze, but I couldn't raise my head to meet eyes with Laney and Blair. The fact was, that still didn't mean he was single, nor did it mean I wanted to go out with him. Or that he even wanted to go out with me. Besides, I had a very important appointment that night, and my love life just might have been changing and all of that chatter would have been for nothing.

CHAPTER 3:
CIDER, SMILES & STOLEN GLANCES

When I signed up for my personal training sessions, they didn't give me an option for which trainer to choose, but I prayed that God would pair Dallas and me together. Walking into the brightly lit gym that night, in my cutest outfit—a coral top with light raspberry leggings and dark purple shoes—I looked like an autumnal paint chip, in a perfect ombre tone. My hair was like my namesake, gingery, and the colors all got bolder from there. I loved it.

"Good evening. I'm here for my 6 p.m. session with a trainer," I said to Megan, who was the night clerk at the desk.

"Hi, Ginger. Let me see who we got for you tonight." She started typing away at her computer while I held my breath, saying a silent prayer. "Looks like you will be with Dallas."

"Thank you, Jesus!" I said quietly under my breath, clasping my hands together in prayer. I knew there was something special about this idea—I just wish I had done it months ago. If I could've gotten his attention earlier, we could have dated all summer. Heck, we could've been engaged by now. My daydreaming of our perfect nuptials was interrupted by Megan.

"He will meet you upstairs in the weight room." As I took the stairs, I hung up my coat and gym bag on a hook beside the weight room entrance. All that I had with me was my water bottle and hair scrunchie. I put my hair in a quick ponytail, checking my reflection in the many mirrors that lined the walls, and waited for Dallas.

There were a few people there working out that night, and I could see another man who looked like Dallas but older, teaching a group aerobics class. That must have been Dallas's older brother, Jace. I had a few more minutes until our session began, so I used the time for reflection and talking to God.

"God, I really like this guy. I pray that if he's the right one for me, doors will open for us."

Dallas entered the room at six on the dot. He looked like he had just come from a workout, sweating head to toe. "Ginger? Hi, I'm Dallas." He held out a sweaty hand to shake mine. I reciprocated the handshake, but I immediately felt I should go wash my hands.

"Hi, Dallas." Wiping my hand on my leggings, I wasn't sure if this was off to a good start or not. But then again, we were in a gym, so I could excuse the sweat.

"What do you want to work on today?" Dallas asked.

"Arms. I'd like to get some more tone to them." Dallas nodded before getting down into a wall-sit and flexing his arm, while putting it under his chin, like a famous sculpture.

"Let's get ripped," he barked before standing back up and loading a barbell.

"Oh, is it cool if we warm up a little first? I get super sore if I don't." Dallas nodded.

"Of course. My mistake: usually, I have my clients do that before I get here, but this is our first session, so you wouldn't know that." His expression was blank as we started doing some stretches. I followed along with him expertly. Then, he brought out the jump ropes. I wasn't as excited about jump roping, mainly because of my clumsiness. "Let's do some double swings to get that heart rate going." It was all Greek to me.

"Sure," I said, not wanting to admit I didn't know what that was. But Dallas caught my bluff.

"That's when it swings twice under your feet in one jump. It's a full body workout *and* my favorite warm up." I was going to protest, as this was a session I was paying for my arms to be tortured, not my pride, when I was immediately disarmed by his handsome, charming smile. His face looked like God had chiseled it by hand. His eyes were bright blue, his suave blonde locks messy from his grueling workout. It may have just been the pheromones talking, but I felt so inspired by his physical appearance, I could have broken out in song.

Small Town Wisdom

Fake it 'til you make it. Unless there's stilts involved.

The double-swing jump roping did not end well. The warmup concluded with a sore spot on my head, nearly split pants, and a partially torn poster off the wall. But after he assured me that he would tape the other half back up later, we began our workout.

First, we went to the barbell, where he took the lead. "Let's start with some overhead presses. These are great for posture." His smile that followed led me to question how straight I was standing. A quick glance in the mirror proved I was pretty slouched, but that was mostly from my stumble earlier. Dallas loaded the barbell and decided I'd start with a set of three, but I couldn't even do one, dropping it to the ground in the middle of my attempt. I looked at the weights, and that was about thirty pounds more than I had ever pressed. Dallas set the barbell back on its ledge and wiped my forehead.

"Whew. I, uh, don't think I can lift any more of those," I laughed with embarrassment, but Dallas kindly nodded and removed the weights, grabbing 10 lb. weights instead of 25 lbs. But with the added weight of the barbell, that was still going to be too much.

"How about we keep it under 60 lbs. total? It's just that my current personal record is about 45 lbs. overhead."

"Oh, sure. You got it. Let's start with thirty and move up slowly in that case." His tone was very kind, but I was starting to feel like a wimp, since that far, I was two for two on the things I hadn't been able to complete. But once the barbell was swapped out for a ten-pound bar, and with one ten-pound weight on each side, I was mastering that movement.

During our entire workout, he watched my form and gave me pointers but didn't ask me a single question about myself. He was very professional, I thought, which brought me much dismay. I'd creeped his social media tons of times and though he had women followers, it appeared that he was single. I decided to start the conversation.

"So, what do you do for fun?" He looked caught off-guard by my question.

"Oh. Uh, basketball, mostly. Or swimming. Me and my buddies are training for a triathlon in the spring. The full Iron Man. Ah, you're doing that wrong, right there. Here, let me show you." He wrapped his now less-sweaty hand over the back of mine, while standing next to me, and slowly lifted my arm into what he considered the perfect rep. "Count to three when you come up, hold, and then count to two on the way down." I did what he said in five more reps, to which he nodded and praised at the end. "High five." I eagerly met his hands with mine, but it was over before it began. And any further attempt I made at conversation seemed to fizzle out quickly. Instead, he turned things back to the workout. "You know, Ginger. . . You should really consider adding creatine to your diet. Focus on lean proteins. No carbs, no sugars. No caffeine, either. It changed my life when I started letting my body wake up naturally rather than focus on stimulants."

"Hey, Dallas." A guy who I'd seen in the gym before walked past the weight room. . Dallas excused himself for a moment.

"My man, Travis." Dallas and Travis slapped hands, which I gathered was some sort of greeting that was in between shaking hands and slapping each other in the face. I set the barbell down after one last intense rep and took the time to take a quick break while he was with his friend. I kept stealing glances over at him as the mirror in front of me showed everything, and I began to creep myself out, so I turned the other direction and faced a wall of dumbbells. Picking up a set of 10 lb. dumbbells, I decided to take initiative and work on some more things, when I heard the conversation come to an end. Travis had said goodbye to Dallas, and someone else had entered a conversation with my dreamy trainer.

I relaxed my intense grip and straightened my posture as I thought it was another gymgoer, but then a particular *drawl* caught my attention. As I turned around, I almost dropped the dumbbells in surprise. It was *Tucker.*

From where he stood, I saw him smiling as he watched me while conversing with Dallas. If I had been able to act cool for even a moment, I would've waved. But I had questions, like why was he there to begin with? Were he and Dallas friends? Or maybe Tucker was dating Megan up front? No, that couldn't be. I remembered Megan was wearing a glitzy diamond ring on her finger. Everything under those lights appeared so dazzling, it was hard to miss. But I just *knew* that man was in a relationship.

Dallas, quickly excusing himself, walked over to a desk near the stairs and returned to hand Tucker an envelope. The men shook hands, and Tucker left. As Dallas returned to me, I was doing the slowest reps I could muster. Any faster and my arms would fall off.

"Sorry about that." Dallas' eyes analyzed everything I was doing, so I could immediately tell he was about to critique my movements. But I didn't have time for that, since my curiosity got the better of me.

"Was that the *pie guy*?" I asked nonchalantly.

"Yeah, the gym is having a fall party with food. Sacrilegious, I know. A little open house to remind them why they should have their memberships here because they can't avoid sweets, I guess. Needless to say, it wasn't my idea. He's going to make us some refreshments, though I don't find anything about simple sugars and refined carbs *refreshing.*"

Favorite Fall Recipes (when on a diet)
One cup whipped topping
2 graham crackers
Oh no, these are delicious together
Finish polishing off the tub and entire box of graham crackers
Repent

At the end of the session, I wasn't ready to admit it, but I felt disappointed. While I couldn't feel my arms at all and was genuinely concerned how I was going to get any work done the next day, it seemed like there was less to Dallas than I thought. He didn't seem very deep or introspective.

His life was fitness. He lived for the gym, and he was very good at his job. While I still had two sessions left, I was beginning to wonder if Dallas has just been a placeholder in my life—a goal for me to obtain or if my feelings for him were real. Did I really want to be with a guy who ran marathons *for fun?* Who never allowed himself to indulge in anything tasty or even have, what I considered was the best part of my day, a cup of coffee? Did I like him or the *idea* of him? I had to give that some thought. What kind of man did I want? More importantly, what kind of man did God want for me? And why did Tucker rattle me so much?

That night as I pulled into my driveway, I slowly walked the lit path to the door of our family's craftsman bungalow. It had been in our family since it was built in 1920, originally purchased by my great grandparents. When my parents inherited it, we quickly outgrew the house, but they managed to hold onto it all of those years by renting it out to traveling nurses. After high school, when I was finishing up my nail program at the beauty school, we agreed that I could take the property tax payments over and live in the house while they moved out of state for my father's career. It was a wonderful start to my adult life, and I was forever grateful for them. Since then, I'd done some upgrades when money allowed, such as new carpet, fresh paint, and wallpaper, and Bruce was able to spray my existing kitchen cabinets a sage green. Afterwards, I installed timeless brass hardware. The home was perfect for me.

The moment I stepped into my cozy home, I kicked off my shoes and locked the door behind me. The extra plush mauve carpet met my tired feet. After taking a shower, layering in my favorite orange plaid flannel pajamas, thick teal socks, and plush pink bathrobe, I made myself a small dinner of leftover zucchini lasagna while I read a devotional and reflected on each word like the savory bites I was taking. As I finished my meal, I wasn't ready to give up on Dallas. I couldn't just turn off my crush. So, he was a little more *sporty* than I realized. He took athletics to the max, and there was a chance that was all there was to him. But if he liked me, wouldn't that make up for it?

The next morning, I awoke to a freezing house. The cold was had arrived; I could feel it coming in through my old windows. I dressed in a lace camisole with my thickest taupe cardigan sweater that had big brown buttons, which reminded me of Oreo cookies. Then, I pulled on my favorite pair of light wash jeans, heavy socks, and shearling boots.. My oversized, peach squash blossom necklace perfectly paired with the look. I may have traded my *Uggs* for peach *Ariat* boots that day, but after all, I was just a girl living in a cowboy world.

Everything was loose on my frame, but I was used to wearing baggier clothes then. I dabbed some soft, peachy makeup on my face and eyes with a little mascara and eyeliner. My stomach growled. I desperately wanted something hearty and fluffy, like a bagel with lox or a fried egg sandwich. But eating like a fawn all year had proven to be a difficult habit to break, especially since I was finally spending time with Dallas, anyway. I scoured the fridge, deciding on an omelet *again.*

As I slowly ate away at the bland breakfast, I recalled how Dallas recommended I give up the remaining traces of sugar and carbs in my diet along with coffee. What was left to enjoy? What was left of *life* without my enjoyable little coffee pick-me-ups? The treat of a bowl of unbuttered popcorn at night? A little extra dollop of peanut butter with my celery? Thoughts of Tucker's sweet treats popped into my head, along with his annoyingly on-point statement about being made in God's image.

I pushed my plate away. Lord, what was I doing? Is this dedication, or *obsessive?* I immediately sought time in the Word, praying for my health of mind and body. I stepped on the scale, revealing I had lost ten pounds that year. Ten pounds I didn't need to lose. I considered how I felt and decided I didn't feel any healthier than I did before my intense, frequent workouts. I certainly wasn't sleeping as soundly, and the crush on Dallas that started innocently was, nearly nine months later, leading me down a dangerous path of disorder. And, instead of feeling empowered, I felt more insecure than ever.

It wasn't time to go to work yet, as my first appointment wasn't for another two hours, so I did my favorite thing to do: take my study Bible to the coffee shop where I would sit in a comfy chair, sip a warm drink, and relish in the rich ambience of fragrant coffee smells. Arriving at *The Pumpkin Perk Cafe* was a bit of a letdown, however, as my favorite seating was already taken. Instead of holing up in a corner, out of sight, I sat right next to the door, catching every single eye that passed and every cold drift the outside brought in with it. The first thing I noticed, however, was the lack of traffic for a Friday morning. Usually, that place was popping. Tucker's truck must have really been putting a damper on business. I was overwhelmed with feelings of self-doubt, distraction, and pondering the mysteries of my heart's desires when I saw Tucker walk in, carrying a handful of his small, pink paper bags.

"Well, good mornin', Ginger." Tucker's kind eyes and sweet drawl met me warmly. Immediately, I felt a little awkward, considering I was there at his competition; but then again, that shop had been there for my entire life, so I brushed that thought aside.

Small Town Wisdom

A man in Wranglers is a reminder that God gave us eyes for a reason.

"Hi, Tucker. What are you up to?" My voice sounded sad. I was still waiting for my coffee but didn't intend on sounding so... defeated.

"I made some samples of my baked goods to see if this cafe wanted to carry them." Something about that guy's availability just didn't sit well with me... He just seemed too kind and nice to be single. Though I'd never really had a solid relationship, I was used to things being much more...difficult, if that was even what was happening there.

"Ginger, Maple Mocha Latte." The barista boomed my coffee order, and as I stood to retrieve it, my arms noticeably struggled to push myself up from the chair. Tucker noticed.

"Hey, I'll get that for you." He waltzed over to the barista, who seemed to be excited to take the pie samples from his hand, and picked up my coffee. The barista had another few words to say to him before he returned, handing me the cup.

"Thank you, Tucker. I think I overdid it at the gym last night. It almost hurts to hold this today." Tucker made a concerned face.

"Well, I better go open up shop. Come see me if you want to try my Maple Mocha Latte." He looked back at the barista, then to me and whispered, "I promise it's better." I had no doubt his was better, as just the scent of that drink gave off burnt espresso fumes. I smiled and waved. When he stepped out the door, he leaned down and picked up a bright red leaf, pulling out a small book from his shirt pocket and pressing it in the pages.

There was a sweetness and masculinity about Tucker that I found intriguing, but I didn't want to look any deeper. Tucker didn't seem like the type of man who didn't already have a lady in his life. He was just too much of a steady, kind type. And he sure had a nice physique from what I could tell: broad and strong. I'd almost bet money he had abs under that flannel. But part of me was looking for an epic love story. Someone I had to earn, like Dallas. I wasn't saying that was right, but I knew if I could get him to love me, then it would have all have been worth it. I was just running out of ideas on how to make that happen.

With thirty minutes until my next appointment, and lackluster coffee consumed, I schlepped over the two blocks to *The Cozy Cuticle.* Laney was already there, wearing a bright pink headband and a chunky checkered sweater with metallic pink cowboy boots. It was absolutely adorable. She was doing the nails of Trina Perry, the owner of Maple Haven's nicest B&B, where Laney held her wedding last year.

"Hello, love," she called out in between telling her client what sounded like the entire, in-depth plot to a book she just read. "And the ending?" She pulled her file off of Trina's nails for dramatic effect, lowering her voice, "He was guilty all along." Trina gasped while Laney nodded. "I know. You just can't be too careful these days in the dating world." As if Laney reminded herself about my love life, she turned to me. "Ginger? Can you be a doll and get me a refill on my coffee? I will return the favor for you later."

"I would love one, too, Ginger. I'll pay for all of us to get one if you don't mind." Trina pulled out a crisp $20 bill.

"Of course, Trina." I looked over at Laney who was sheepishly smiling at me. "What drink do you want?" I asked.

"I'll take the daily special. That's what Laney got, and she loves it. By the way, it's so cute that you two like each other." Her words stopped me in my tracks. What had Laney let on about now? Being on my best, customer-friendly behavior, I looked at her with a smile.

"And what makes you say that, Trina? It's news to me." We both shot a look at Laney who put her hands up in the air.

"Hey, I'm just reading between the lines here. Don't be mad at me because I'm just the first one to see it." She shook the bottle of taupe polish in her hand.

"He **did** seem very cute from what I saw this morning, Ginger. I only caught a glance. Much kinder than that gym guy you like, too." Yes, it seemed that everyone knew about my feelings for Dallas. Except Dallas.

"Yeah, he's fine on paper. I don't really know anything about him, though. Besides, Dallas and I have been working out together." Laney scoffed at my statement.

"You mean you *hired* him to work out with you, Ginger. Dallas is as emotionally rich as a protein bar, and if his skull is too thick to see what a wonderful woman you are, then I think you should give someone else a chance instead of just waiting around for Dallas." Laney was right about one thing: Dallas didn't seem to have much going on in the emotions department. But this was starting to sound like a broken record, and I didn't know how much longer I could stand it.

"You know, Ginger, sometimes, appearing a tad more *unavailable* or *mysterious* spikes interest for men. I'm not saying that it's a good thing, and I certainly don't think you want to play games, but maybe taking the focus off of Dallas and getting to know another man would help the situation overall. It could certainly bring you more clarity. Being too available to Dallas might actually be pushing him away. Make him miss you a little, you catch my drift?" Trina's idea needed a little refining, but it was solid gold, nonetheless. I considered how unattainable Dallas was and how that made me work harder to get his attention; and how uncomplicated Tucker seemed, which made any possible interest fade. She was totally right.

"So... I should make Dallas jealous... by pretending to be interested in someone else?" I stammered out. Both Trina and Laney started shaking their heads.

"No, no. Not fake crushes: that will be messy and hurtful. That's not what I meant. I mean, try getting to know someone sincerely." Trina was backpedaling, but I got the gist of it. I nodded and left for the coffee.

CHAPTER 4:
TWO STEPPIN' INTO TROUBLE

Golden leaves swirled around the truck in every direction as I stood in line. Two people were getting gorgeous slivers of freshly baked pies in front of me. My mouth watered uncontrollably. Tucker smiled at me as he waited for the customers to pay, counting out their cash. Part of me felt racked with anxiety—what if Tucker said no to my pitch? The other part felt excited to be taking action in my life.

"Ginger. Here for that Maple Mocha?" Tucker cheerfully asked. I'd already forgotten all about the coffees, but I remembered I was holding a twenty-dollar bill.

"Oh, yes. And, um, Laney and her client would both like the daily coffee special?" My nerves kicked in. Tucker pointed to a sign on his truck's counter and laughed. Today's special *was* the Maple Mocha Latte.

"You inspired me today. Three coffees, coming right up." He turned to make the drinks, and I hesitated over my words. But

I had to remember the ultimate goal: Dallas. Trina was right; I should get to know this new man in town. It would be the friendly thing to do. The *Christian* thing. We are to be charitable and kind, right? With the Fall Festival coming up in just next week, maybe Tucker could even be my date. Ha! That could be the perfect showdown as there was not a soul in that town that didn't attend. I knew for a fact Dallas would be there because he usually won the Maple Mile Fun Run. *Though I didn't think there was anything fun about running.* Tucker was almost done steaming the milk. As I wrestled with my thoughts, I said a silent prayer for my intentions to be pure in all of that, even if they didn't feel that way then.

"So, Tucker..." I trailed off, but he perked right up and came to chat on the counter while the espresso dripped into the cups.

"Yes, Ginger?" His earnest, warm personality made me feel things I couldn't pinpoint.

"I saw you picking up a leaf earlier. Do you like. . .collect them or something?" Such a lame conversation starter, but I went with it.

"Oh, yeah, I kind of do." He pulled out the little book from his pocket. It was a small book of Christian devotions. He motioned for me to look through the pages, and most of them had a beautiful, perfect leaf pressed between them. "The leaves here are so lovely. I'm from Northern Wyoming, and they are already dried out by Labor Day because of our wind. I just can't resist but keep souvenirs of my time here." I didn't intend to be intrigued, but I was.

"How long *are* you here for, Tucker?" A small detail that was certainly important to my plan of getting to know him and possibly our coupling up platonically for the festival.

"I don't know, honestly. I have to have my residency here through the season, since I intend to compete in the pie bake-off, of course. The city granted me use of this spot until the first part of December. I'm staying at that little motel on the corner—you know the one?" I nodded.

"*Whispering Pines Lodge.* Cute place. Laney's husband Bruce helped with their remodel last year. I actually got to weigh in on the paint colors," I smiled at him knowingly, putting my hand to my chest in honor. The whole place had been gutted and revamped into a hip spot to stay.

"Well—is that so? I guess I have you to thank for a refreshing cinnamon wall color—a major opposite from most soulless, depressing motel rooms." I laughed, feeling a buzz of confidence. "It's just a temporary spot. I personally prefer a little more elbow room," Tucker smiled. "I'm used to having nothing but horses for neighbors."

"That sounds better than my neighbors. Think year-round pink flamingos in the yard. At least they put lights on them for Christmas."

"You know, I actually wanted to come say hi last night when I saw you working out at the *Maple Muscle Gym*, but I didn't want to interrupt your session with Dallas," Tucker said as his back was to me.

"Is that so?" I said, knowing full well he had, as I saw him, too.

"It looked like a pretty intense workout, if I do say so myself." He turned, handing me the first coffee with a knowing expression. "You certainly were taking it very seriously." I had a feeling that my motives had been exposed, and it didn't feel good.

"Okay, fine." I let out a sigh. Holding all of this in had been exhausting, anyway. Besides, I had no feelings or intentions of liking Tucker, so it didn't even matter if I came clean. "I am trying to get someone that I like to notice me. He works there. So, I signed up for lessons, and yes, I am trying very hard to get his attention and so far, all I've gotten from him was the recommendation to give up the last thing I enjoy in my life—

coffee!" I buried my head in my hands until he turned back around to grab the other coffees.

"I see," Tucker mumbled.

"And now, a client just told me that I should get to know you so that he will think I'm taken, and I will finally get his attention."

"Is that so?"

"Ugh. You're not going to tell anyone what I'm up to, are you?" I whispered, looking behind me to see if anyone else heard my confession.

"No, of course not." I released the breath I was holding.

"Okay, great. Thank you," I said, smiling.

"But, it's not a bad idea that your client had about portraying interest in me." My eyes widened. "In fact, I was wondering if you could help me with something that's also a little... discreet." What on earth could this be?

Hesitating, I considered turning and running away from this entire conversation. "Oh, um. . .sure?"

Tucker nodded. "There's something I'm after, too. You know the pie bake-off? Well, it turns out, the judges have a bit of a bias towards out-of-towners like myself. It doesn't matter that I'm from Wyoming, either. They still see me as a non-resident who is staking claim here just long enough to enter. Rightfully so, sure. Normally, I wouldn't mind. But it seems they've caught wind of. . .something else. That doesn't make my chances look so good. That's where maybe you could help me." My mind went in a million directions.

"I don't know any of the judges personally, Tucker. How could I possibly help you?" I pleaded.

"My image. If they thought I had a nice local girl as my sweetheart, well..." he trailed off. "They may just overlook some of the *other* things." I had so many questions. First of which, what other things? I realized I had said that out loud when he started laughing. His eyes lit up under his brown Stetson hat. "Nothing on my record, I promise." He held his hands up like I was holding him at gun point. "I didn't do anything, but rather, called out someone who was in the wrong..."

"What if Dallas comes around, but I have a 'fake' boyfriend already?" I was genuinely concerned how this might affect my pursuance of Dallas.

"Oh, so it *is* Dallas?" Tucker stiffened up but cracked a smile.

"Yeah, so what?" I felt defensive, and I didn't know why.

"No reason. It's just...he's a little *emotionally detached*, don't you think?"

"How would you know? Didn't you just move here?" I raised my eyebrows at him, knowing full well he was right.

"I'm sorry, darlin'. That was out of line. You're right, and it's none of my business." He retrieved a matching pink carrying tray, put the coffees inside and added little plugs to the coffee lids so they would stay piping hot.

"Thank you." His politeness was refreshing, though I didn't care to admit that. He was a true gentleman so far in our fake arrangement, or whatever that was.

"Then, do we have a deal? You pretend to be my girl until the pie bake-off, help me taste test recipes, and in return, I will help you accomplish your mastermind plan to get Dallas?"

"Woah, now. Since when does eating pies have anything to do with *improving your image*?" My acrylic nails cut through the air while I used air quotes. I wasn't about to blow my diet for that cowboy.

Ginger's Polished Thoughts

When a man sees a woman with acrylic nails, why does his back suddenly itch?

"How else will I know which recipes are right? I have a lot riding on this win, Ginger. It sure would help if I had a taste tester for my samples that I'm creating. If you do that for me, taking bites of my pies here and there and giving open, honest feedback, you can tell Dallas whatever you want about us to, uh, make him jealous, or whatever."

"Fake date," I hollered, putting my finger up in the air. I contemplated blowing my diet and carb-cutting lifestyle to meet his demands, weighing out the pros and cons. What could one bite of a delicious pie really do to my physique? "And you have a deal." I held out my hand to shake his, which he reciprocated, and took my tray of coffee back to the salon.

"Have a good day, sweetheart," Tucker called out behind me, already playing up the boyfriend thing. For a moment, it felt really good to have someone, even if it wasn't real.

Walking back into *The Cozy Cuticle* with a drink tray in hand, Laney immediately knew something was up.

"Thanks, smiley," she said as she took two of the coffees, setting one down in front of Trina and taking a gulp of the other. "It's even better the second time around." She put her hand on Trina's shoulder as she examined the dryness of her French manicure. "You're good to go, girly."

"Thank you, Laney. And Ginger, for getting the coffee." Trina held up her cup to me in thanks.

"Oh, I almost forgot, here's your change." I handed her the remains from her twenty-dollar bill, but she waived it off.

"Put it in your girls' coffee fund. We can't lose Tucker and his creative ideas. I hope we can all support him as much as possible."

"No doubt we will, Trina. Thank you," I said, as Laney cocked an eyebrow.

"We?" She said as soon as Trina was out the door.

"Yes, we need to support...*my boyfriend*." I almost couldn't say it with a straight face, but I knew she was going to see right through it anyway. I didn't care. I felt reckless.

"You mean, fake love interest? Don't tell me you pitched that idea to sweet, sweet Tucker. He's far too nice to get wrapped up into some plot to win over a horse bro." Laney was harsh, but as always, right. Still, it wasn't like that. It was his idea. She wasn't there when it happened.

"No, I mean, for real. It was his idea. We are giving it a shot. Everyone was right; he's a great guy." I sat down at my station and started filing away at the edge of one of my pink acrylics, giving an air of mystery, like Trina had said. It only ramped Laney up more. Then Blair walked in, and I knew this would be the real ringer.

"You'll never guess what just happened, sis." Laney dug right in, and Blair's eyes widened.

"What?" She ran over, leaning on my nail table, looking at us both.

"Why don't you tell her, Ginger?"

"Tucker and I are dating." It was a crazy statement to say for the second time in five minutes, when just yesterday morning, I had made it clear I wanted nothing to do with him.

"How? When? How?" Blair moved her face to Laney and me on repeat, waiting for answers.

"It just sort of happened." I shrugged it off. "When I went out there to get us coffee."

"I don't believe you." Laney straightened and crossed her arms.

"Go ask him. See for yourself." I motioned to the truck, knowing Laney was crazy enough to do just that. She picked up her coffee and shook it.

"Fine, I'm due for a refill anyway!"

"Fine!" I yelled back. Blair was still looking at me with disbelief. As Laney stomped out of the salon in her larger-than-life metallic pink cowboy boots, her blonde hair bouncing as she walked, I couldn't help but smirk.

"Is this real, Ginger?" Blair, always the sweeter one of the two, asked. I didn't want to lie, but thankfully, I didn't have to. Two clients walked in, Mazzy and Lily. High school best friends in their senior year. Blair walked over and greeted the girls.

"Can we get full sets? Like this," they showed Blair a photo on a cell phone.

"Oh, how fun is that! Yes, we can do that. Ginger here is actually the pro at nail art scarecrows. The smaller the better." Blair winked at me, and I knew this was payback for her clearly not believing me about Tucker. I gladly took the punishment, as Laney returned to the salon, expression softened.

"Well?" Blair asked while the girls were getting seated.

"I guess it's true. They both corroborate the story, anyway." Laney looked at me with squinted eyes. "It's just a little...convenient, wouldn't you say? Right after Trina gives you that idea and everything."

"What idea?" Blair asked. The girls were too immersed with picking out their base color for their fall themed nails.

"Oh, Trina Perry was in here a little bit ago and said that Ginger should make herself less available to get Dallas's attention, by getting to know another man." Blair gasped.

"Ginger—you would *never* do that to such a great guy— right?" I rolled my eyes.

"Look, guys—I love you both. But can we drop this conversation for a bit?" I motioned to the girls who had finalized their polish colors, and Laney and Blair agreed. Turning back to Laney and Blair, I whispered, "And may I remind you that we know *very little* about this man with the pink coffee cups?" Blair shrugged, but Laney was the holdout. I knew she wouldn't give in, even if she agreed with me.

"Fine—as in, let's put a pin in this until later. I have Samantha coming in anytime now, anyway." Laney gave me a flatlined look, still suspicious, but I saw a smile behind her expression. She was hopeful that it was real.

Samantha James, a young woman who had recently become a real estate agent at a firm specializing in multi-million-dollar cattle ranches and commercial properties, blew into the salon with a sharp gust of wind. Her dark red hair was perfectly curled, half-up in a small clip. She had bright blue eyes and pillowy lips, with freckles covering her cheeks. She was a horse girl through and through, having been raised on a ranch just outside of town, and she came from a long line of old money. I always tried my hardest to not compare myself to other women, but Samantha was just so beautiful that I felt insecure in her presence. Saying a quick prayer under my breath that those worldly feelings would leave me, I put my focus back on my customer.

"There's my girl," Laney smiled as she turned on the water for Samantha's pedicure. While the two women conversed, their conversation was drowned out by my deep concentration as I drew the heavily detailed nail art on my clients' fingers. My ears perked up towards the end of Samantha's pedicure as I heard a familiar name.

"His name is Tucker Callahan. And I know—" Laney's voice cut-off mid-sentence. I looked over, catching Samantha's gaze that felt more like a glare if anything. I then noticed she was holding a pink cup. Ahh. She's met my *pretend* boyfriend. But what else happened? I held my breath so I could put all of my energy toward listening into the rest of their exchange.

"He's already off the market, actually," Laney tried to whisper, but between the nail drill Blair was using, the water going in the pedicure tub Laney was cleaning as she prepared to paint Samantha's nails, and the music we were playing, it wouldn't have done her any good to whisper. We were all accustomed to talking louder than normal when in the salon. But Samantha, on the other hand, was quiet as a mouse. I forgot that Laney could read lips better than anyone I knew. I looked over at the perfect time: Laney was motioning over her shoulder to me with a nail file in her hand. Samantha's gaze *was* a full-blown glare then. And I didn't know how I felt about it, but certainly, some guilt was involved.

As our clients filtered in and out the rest of the day, Laney, Blair and I barely had any time to talk about anything besides the task at hand. For that, I was thankful. I really hadn't thought much beyond Tucker and our fake dating for my benefit of Dallas's attention, but the more I reflected with what I had conspired, the worse I felt. By the end of the day, I decided I would come clean with Laney and Blair and immediately call it off with Tucker, along with a deep apology. But before I could do either, something caught me by surprise.

"Hi, Ginger." Tucker came into the salon, his outfit of orange plaid and Carhartt pants blending in with our autumn window displays. He tipped his cowboy hat as he greeted the ladies, the muscle tone of his arms appearing more than subtle as he did it. He was a walking fall catalog for a farm store, in the best way possible. With one arm behind his back, he grinned at me.

"Tucker. How nice to see you." I stood as I awkwardly greeted him, though I didn't want to admit just *how* nice it felt to see him. To be *seen* by a man, facade or not. The salon went silent as I excused myself from my last acrylic fill of the day and walked over to him. *Do I hug him? Do I shake his hand?* Sure, my plan was to call this off, but not there. Not like that, in front of several members of the community. It would be done in private and out of respect for him; however, I would greet him like a girlfriend should right at that second.

"These reminded me of you." Tucker pulled out a stunning pink and golden hued bouquet of flowers from behind his back. They were wrapped in pink paper and tied with a piece of twine. They were a beautiful variety; some flowers I'd never even seen before.

"Thank you, Tucker. I love them." I leaned in to experience the intoxicating aroma of fresh cut florals.

"I was down at the farmers' market, picking up some more eggs and fresh cream when I saw them, and they reminded me of you. I couldn't resist."

"That was so thoughtful of you, Tucker," Laney chimed in, placing a vase with water on the counter of the salon. "And might I add, they will look beautiful in Ginger's home." Laney was right about that; those warm tones really popped in my freshly painted kitchen. Tucker smiled.

"Well, I better get back to it. I'm trying out a new recipe right now, about to take it out of the oven actually, so I'll have something for you to try tonight. Stop by when you're done here."

His smile turned clever, and he gave me a wink before leaving the salon, the colorful leaves blowing past the door on his way out.

"He's a keeper, that one," Franny Chan, the owner of the Maple Haven grocery store chimed in.

"I know. They just started dating *today,* if you can believe it." Laney added, as she sat back down to finish Franny's nails, giving me a look as she did.

"He sure knows how to make a girl feel special," Franny said. "My Frank used to do all sorts of things to get my attention back in the day. Once, when I was working at a clothing shop, he came in and let us girls sell him a whole outfit. Frank wore those bell bottoms for a year before I finally admitted that I hated the look. Thankfully, he switched to polyester pants and has worn them ever since." We all giggled at the thought of Frank Chan, infamously shorter than Franny by almost a foot, wearing bell bottoms. "His persistence paid off, though. I got to know him through friendship, rather than a high-pressure dating scenario. And he's made me the happiest woman in the world for forty-some years."

Ginger's Polished Thoughts
A nail salon has more romantic stories than a bookstore.

"What was that about Tucker having things for you to try, Ginger?" Blair chimed in after everyone was quieting down following Franny's story.

"Oh, nothing much. I'm going to help him taste-test some recipes, that's all. He wants to enter the pie bake-off at the Pumpkin Stampede." Laney and Blair both looked at me in shock.

"That's fantastic, Ginger!" Blair hollered, with Laney in agreement of the sentiment.

"Yeah, I guess. He's really excited about the contest." I finished filing the acrylic nails of my client, Rachel Smith, and got ready for her gel color, while the girls went on about it.

"Now that you're breaking your diet, finally! And indulging in Tucker's baked goods." Laney winked at me. "One bite, and I think you'll fall in love with him."

"If I was thirty years younger, I think I'd fall in love with him just for knowing his way around an oven," Mabel Green, Blair's client, chimed in. "I never did find myself in the kitchen. It would have been nice to have a man helping me out in that department."

"Here, here," Rachel Smith raised her pink cup in sentiment. "It's just as easy to fall in love with a man who knows how to cook, Ginger." I nodded and smiled back, but inside, my mind was racing with thoughts of Dallas, Tucker, and the mess I'd just created. Word was spreading quickly since Tucker had made such a public display of affection for me, though it was based on a ruse. So, the next time I'd see all of those ladies, I'd be explaining how we were no longer together. The less people involved, the better this would pan out.

As we finished our last clients of the day, the sun was setting, and it was a colorful masterpiece of cotton candy-colored clouds in the sky. While I wrestled with my revelation earlier of telling them the truth about Tucker and me, my strength and bravery was waning. I decided to let the day be the perfectly fun day that it was and come clean later. So, while Laney and Blair went out the back door of the salon to their cars, I offered to lock up the front since I was going to stop by Tucker's food truck.

"Have fun," Laney smiled, either too tired from the long, busy day or accepting of my new relationship status.

"Thank you." I told both of them goodnight, stopping at our front desk before departing. I thought it best to write out the terms of our agreement and review it with him again, because his showing up earlier with the flowers was very kind and generous, but it was equally unexpected. I jotted a few things down, hit the lights, and went out the front door, locking it. The second I turned around to face Tucker's truck, I was hit with the most heavenly scents. Cinnamon, butter, sugar...pumpkin. It was a feast for my senses, and my mouth was watering as I walked up. Tucker was waiting for me.

"Hi." He looked at me, with his hands on his waist; the beige apron he had on over his clothes peppered with food. "Don't mind me; my mixer went rogue this afternoon." He undid the back tie of his apron and hung it on a hook in the back of his truck.

"Good evening, Tucker. I'm here to hold up my end of the bargain." I threw my hands up in the air expectantly.

"Thank you, Ginger. I was thinking, would you like a tour of my truck?" His question threw me off. I thought I'd be halfway through the delicious, scented pie right at that time and halfway to blowing my diet.

"Sure, why not?" I looked both directions to see how to enter, while he pointed to the back. The door swung open, and he reached for my hands, as if it had a little bit of a step to it. I accepted, and he pulled me inside. I was immediately impressed by his strength; some muscle definition was apparent under his layers of plaid, but I was starting to think there was more to him than pie.

"This is where it all happens," Tucker beamed as he showed me his espresso machine, oven, and coolers on the left of the truck. On the right side was his counter and underneath, out of the customers' sight, was a large wooden prep area with lots of evidence of baking. Flour was scattered all along it where some fresh dough was being rolled out. An empty pie pan was waiting for it, while another pie pan had a fresh crust laid inside of it.

"It's much bigger inside than I expected." Along the right side of it were recipes; each one held up to the wall with a magnet. And lastly, there was a photograph of a woman. I found myself looking at it a little longer than to go unnoticeable.

"That's my sister, Tara. She died last year." I felt the weight of his loss, unable to form words meaningful enough.

"I'm so sorry, Tucker." He nodded.

"Thank you. It's been a challenge. This was all her idea. The truck, the recipes, and all-things-pink, which I feel a little silly about now, but the customers love it." He shrugged. "We were going to do it together. While she still could. But her cancer progressed faster than we ever expected." I teared up while looking at her photo. She was so full of life, full of beauty.

"What an unimaginable loss. But it's really beautiful that you are doing it in her honor now." I felt overwhelmed with emotions for him and gave Tucker a hug. It was rather mild and over before it started, but it was a friendly squeeze to let him know I cared. And I was starting to really care, more than I could admit to myself.

"Thank you. It's my 'why' for the pie contest, too. I think she would have really been excited about it. I knew Maple Haven did lots of fall things here, but the contest was just an added bonus." Tucker ran his fingers through his curly hair.

"On that note. . .I wrote out the things that we both agreed to earlier. . .just in case, you know, you had any questions about it," I smiled at him sheepishly. This whole thing was starting to feel very awkward to discuss. Tucker took the piece of paper I held out and analyzed it.

"Let's see. . . Pie sampling and honest feedback... Fake date for improving Tucker's image and making Dallas jealous..." He trailed off. "You forgot one thing." He looked at me and handed back the paper. I pulled out the pen from my pocket and clicked it.

"What's that?" I was ready to write anything down.

"No falling in love." I pulled back in surprise.

"Oh, yeah, sure. '*No falling in love*' has been added. Anything else?" I asked.

"I feel like it needs a title. It's not so much a contract, per se. It's more of an agreement that you will help me with honest feedback to win the pie bake-off, and my presence will hopefully help you win, uh, the guy."

"It's a pumpkin pie *pact,* if you will." I folded up the paper and slid it into my jeans pocket.

"There it is," Tucker nodded. "Now, enough about that. Let's have you taste the pie. Tonight's selection is a mashup between my sister's favorite pie recipe that she used to make in high school for the bake sale, and a little bit of my own flavor. I'm calling it: Pumpkin Praline." He took it out of the cooler and cut me a slender slice.

"That looks so good, but I won't eat the whole thing." Tucker graciously nodded and put a dollop of whipped cream next to the pie. He handed me the pink plate, taking a larger slice for himself and motioned to the exit.

"There are some chairs out back for us. It's such a beautiful sunset, I thought we could enjoy it while we discussed the flavors of this contest-contender." He helped me back out of the truck, and we went around the back. There, set up under two rows of twinkling lights, was a small picnic table and a heat lamp. It was very cozy, and I admired his ingenuity.

"How creative that you can utilize this space out here." Since it was a dead-end street, and the closest building other than my nail salon was an insurance office, it was quite peaceful for that time of night. We both got settled into the picnic table, and he had to remind me it was time to eat the pie. I hesitated, hovering my fork over the firm, plump pumpkin filling. I reminded myself that one bite wasn't going to magically undo all of the work I'd been putting in for Dallas to notice me, and put a small amount of pie on my fork.

"I don't mean to be nitpicky, but the crust is also a part of the pie…" Tucker was right about that. Fine. I put an ample amount of both the crust and the pie on my fork and took a bite.

To say it was life-changing was an understatement: That pie gave life to my body. From the sweetness of the praline bits to the buttery smoothness of the crust, the indulgence of the pumpkin pie was unmatched. The notes of cinnamon were vibrant and electrifying, plus a subtle zest of something else that I couldn't quite put my finger on. I'd never experienced food like that before. Ever. And I told him all of that as I devoured the entire slice.

Favorite Fall Recipes (hack)

One-part gluttonous treat

Consume while wearing workout clothes, and the calories don't count

Will also burn calories if done while standing over kitchen sink

"This is the best pie I've ever had. In my life. And I *love* pumpkin pie." I tore through the piece and found myself wishing there was more. He read my mind.

"Want the rest of mine? It's all blending together for me at this point," He laughed, setting his untouched piece of pie down next to me.

"I better not," I said, but I did have another gym session later that night, so what was the harm just that one time? Besides, the pumpkin was healthy. The rest of it would even out. I ate half of that slice before the sugar went to my head, and I felt like I could run a marathon. "What else have you been keeping from me?" I asked him.

"I'm pretty sure you are the one who has been abstaining from baked goods. I've been offering them at every turn."

"You're right, and I'm sorry. I think I just got a little in my head for a while. Trying to be as fit as I could and all. But now, I'm starting to see that 'balance' that Laney and Blair have been hammering into my head. They were right. This is good. And worth it." I smiled at Tucker, and he looked at me. I wasn't the best reader of situations, but I felt that Tucker wanted to put his arm around me. And for that moment, I hoped he would. But a small burst of wind came down the corridor of the street and the moment passed.

"So, you were talking about your image? I mean, I don't mean to press, but...you've got me really curious." I licked the plastic fork until every trace of the plate was clean.

Tucker nodded. "Before I left the rodeo circuit, I was in pretty deep, you could say. The rodeo stock contractor, the people who put the whole thing on in my town? Well, they really took me under their wing. At first, it was amazing; they had me over almost every night for dinner before the rodeo, sent me lavish gifts, and always let me take the best horse in the show, instead of making me draw it out of a hat like everyone else. I just chalked it up to God shining down on me. And I sure enjoyed the attention." Tucker took a sip of his coffee.

"Well, the night I quit rodeo for good; I had made it to NFR in Vegas. The stock contractors flew me out in their private jet. It was so lavish and amazing to travel like that. Right before I go on, the wife of the owner made a pass at me. I'm talking very apparent; no mistaking this was her intention all along. I turned her down pretty brazenly—not only was she a married woman, but I was just 19 years old. She was close to three times my age. It felt *more* than wrong... Predatory? Premeditated? Like she had been grooming me for this very thing all along? Anyway...this very much upset her. She went into a rage, making a huge deal, saying how I came on to her. She started screaming and yelling, drawing attention to everyone around us. I was shut out of the fold *fast.* I should have left right then and there, but I didn't. I decided since I was already there at the NFR, I should compete. Right?" He looked at me expectantly. I shrugged, nodding.

"Yeah, geez. The NFR? That's amazing."

"It turned out to be a very bad decision for me, as the sweetheart deal was off. Word traveled fast, and I got to the chutes, and they made me draw a number for it. I ended up getting the horse that was known to be absolutely crazy. *Insane Membrane* was this horse's nickname; I kid you not. It all felt... intentional. I had a feeling if I dumped all the numbers for horses, every single one would be for that one because they wanted me gone now. And even if I managed to stay upright for eight seconds, my career would have still been gone because they had the power to say so. But the kicker?"

"You did the ride anyway?" I asked.

"Yes, I guess I was feeling wronged and stubborn. Like I had something to prove. And that's when God taught me some humility." My thoughts raced as I pictured him riding a stallion on the worldwide stage at NFR.

"So, what happened?"

"The ride didn't go well, to say the least. In the aftermath, the stock contractors tried to say I had been drinking, which was disproved by a blood test taken by the rodeo medic, thankfully. I've never had a drop of alcohol in my life, and after that accusation failed, it went right back to me coming on to the wife. But, I have no regrets now. All of that is just history; part of my story. And it led me here, to Maple Haven. Where maybe I can have a fresh start in this new passion of mine that I wouldn't have discovered if it hadn't been for all the things I've lost." Tucker smiled and put his hand on my shoulder as I gazed at him in shock. He had really been through so much, and now more than ever, he needed the upper hand. Tucker truly needed help with his image. I just didn't know if I could do it. "Well, I better close up shop tonight. Thank you for holding up your end of the bargain." Tucker smiled as he spoke.

"Yeah, about that, Tucker." My feelings were all over the place. "I don't know if I want to do this. I mean, I don't want anyone to get hurt." I wished right then that I had given some thought before I opened my mouth since my words weren't coming out right.

"So, don't hurt me, and I won't hurt you," Tucker proclaimed.

"Everyone in town loves your truck and everything you make." I crossed my arms. "I feel like this ruse is going to get us into a tangle we can't get out of. Somehow, some way," I said defiantly. "And with all of the attention you're getting from the ladies... What if our *arrangement* keeps you from meeting the woman of your dreams?" He shook his head and let out a laugh.

"First of all: You're my taste tester, remember?" Tucker held up the pie plates before discarding them into a trash receptacle.

"Yeah, I know. But that's not helping you that much, is it? C'mon. You *know* this stuff is good. Better than good. Unreal. Magical. Heavenly. Divinely inspired." I watched Tucker look down to his feet, expecting him to agree with me and call this whole thing off.

"Second of all, I ain't worried about nothing, darlin'. Because here's the thing about God: His plans? We can't run from them. Now, I'm not saying He ain't up there scratching His chin and feeling pretty annoyed with me right now for setting this whole thing up. I've never been that good at not getting involved; you know what I mean?" He looked at me knowingly.

"Yeah, I'm a bit of a control freak myself. Got tired waiting around for things to happen naturally and... Yep. Go on."

"Well, God knows my intentions here. You and I are after two goals that are different, but also the same. We are chasing what we think is ours. And God has the option of opening or closing those doors for us. And believe me, when He wants to shut a door, that baby will slam shut faster than a motel door on its hinges. So, no. I'm not worried about missing out on anything."

"Okay, mystery man. Whatever you want to do," I smiled, still tasting the dessert on my tongue. "By the way, other than the cinnamon, what was that little zest I was tasting in the pie?" Tucker beamed, revealing his nice, white teeth.

"That's my secret ingredient."

CHAPTER 5:
PUMPKIN PATCH PICKIN'

That night as I rolled into the gym parking lot, I was filled with the vigor that only sugar can bring. Greeting Megan, she alerted me that Dallas was already waiting for me in the weight room. I took the stairs two at a time, with my ponytail bouncing buoyantly with each step. Dallas was standing at the weight machines, and he must have heard the pep in my step because he turned his head all the way to greet me.

"Hey, Ginger," he said, looking at me up and down. "How are you?" The first time he had asked me anything somewhat personal, and yet it felt like a parent asking me if my room was clean when it was in fact, not. I had cheated on my diet, and I didn't want him to know, but felt like he could tell just by looking at me. I smirked to myself when I realized I had zero regrets and was looking forward to the next pie tasting.

"I'm great; thanks for asking. So, what are we doing tonight? Legs, arms, abs?" He looked surprised at my question and took a moment to regain his train of thought.

"Let's see. . . I have us down here for legs tonight, since we did arms last time. Does that work for you?" He scanned his clipboard while he waited for me to answer.

"Sure thing. I'm ready." I looked back at him, and his eyes were locked on me.

"What's different about you today?" I knew it: he could sense I had just consumed sugar and carbs.

"Nothing new." Well, if I was *really* going to do this, it was now or never. "I just started seeing someone." Dallas looked at me like he was searching for the answers to the universe. I couldn't tell if he was making a scowl or smiling.

"Is that so?" was all he could muster out.

"Yep. Oh, and I totally blew my diet. He's actually a pretty fantastic baker. So, that might be a problem." I didn't know why I told him that, but it felt good to come clean, even if the relationship itself was a ruse. Maybe it was the sugar, or maybe it was the reminder that other men existed outside of Dallas, but I hadn't felt that bold in years, if ever.

"Well in that case, we better get you a good workout in." Dallas wasn't smiling, but he was paying extra attention to my every movement as we started the workout. The best part? How his not-so-subtle questions were woven in. "So, where did you meet this guy?"

"He parked his dessert truck outside our nail salon. The girls I work with kind of forced me to go talk to him. It was sort of a setup, when I think about it."

"Is this the guy from that *pumpkin* truck who is making all of my clients go off their diets this week?" Dallas crossed his arms. "That Megan ordered from the other night?"

"Yeah, that's the one. He's pretty irresistible." I didn't mean it in the sense that it came out, but I wasn't sure what to say next. I didn't want Dallas to think there wasn't a chance for him. "The treats, I mean."

"Well, if I meet him, I'm going to thank him for the job security. It's been a long time since we've had something that people couldn't resist. It's been seven years since the frozen yogurt place closed, and man, did that place make me a fortune trying to help people burn all of those extra calories off." Dallas was laughing under his breath, but something about his demeanor changed. As we went through the rest of my workout routine, I tried to enjoy the attention from him, but he was looking at me with an intensity that I wasn't sure about.

After the last set of grueling leg presses, Dallas stiffened up.

"So, Ginger. You work at the nail salon, right?" he asked.

"I own it, along with my two best friends," I said. "Why do you ask?"

"I've been training for this triathlon, and I've been having some issues with my feet."

"Do you need to see a podiatrist?" I asked, not sure what he was getting at. He shook his head.

"Nah, I don't think so. This is more of an ingrown nail situation. Can you help me with that?" Technically, yes. Though it wasn't really my idea of a dream date, I supposed I would have liked to spend time with him outside of the gym. Just maybe not dealing with a rogue toenail.

"I might be able to help. Call the salon and make an appointment."

"Yeah, okay. Could I, uh, get your number?" My face blushed uncontrollably. Was that it? Was he asking me for my digits or still on the topic of his feet? I didn't let myself get excited just in case it was the latter.

"Sure." And I gave it to him.

Small Town Wisdom

He spent a lot of time typing on his phone afterwards, while I awkwardly stood there. Eventually, I heard dinging as he kept typing away.

"Sorry, I'm in one of those group chats for my triathlon training. We're meeting at dawn tomorrow." He slid his phone back in his pocket.

"Are you starting a revolution, or training for a race?" I asked. If I was getting up at dawn, it was because I had found *that* good of a deal on a flight. It would never have been for fitness of any kind. As Dallas stood across from me, I noticed a shift in his posture turned into more of a *perch.* It became pretty apparent that he was flexing his muscles. As much as I liked him, I knew that was my cue. I had him right where I wanted him. Didn't I?

As I left the gym, my phone buzzed. It was probably Dallas, hitting me up for that pedicure. I laughed thinking what Laney and Blair would think as he waltzed into our salon. We didn't often get men in, but it did happen sometimes. Though I didn't mind doing men's feet, the best part was the polish and the thick dollop of topcoat and hearing about their lives. Men were notoriously more reserved, not sharing very much if at all.

When I pulled into my driveway and turned the key in my ignition to off, I checked my phone. It wasn't Dallas, but instead, it was Tucker.

"Ginger, it's Tucker. I am delivering pies tomorrow to the pumpkin patch and was wondering if you'd like to join me? No obligation if you're busy, of course."

The pumpkin patch? I hadn't been there in years, despite it being such a major part of my community; the idea sounded fun. I didn't have plans, and my last appointment was earlier in the day. I was completely available.

"I'd like that. Thanks for the invite." I hit send and hurried inside, moving my legs faster than comfortable after that tough training session, and started to scour my closet for the perfect pumpkin patch outfit. After I found a darling orange sweater, a chunky brown belt, and bell bottom jeans with sunflowers on the bottom of the legs, I excitedly laid the outfit out. I would need the perfect pair of boots, as I walked to the hallway closet where I had a whole shelf full. I lived there alone, why not utilize the entire space? I scoured the closet full of colorful cowgirl boots: Some went up to the knee, some only the ankle. My favorite was mid-calf, but all of them I loved. I had almost every color of the rainbow and settled on a pair of *Dingo* mid-calf boots that looked like yellow denim. They were ultra comfortable, and I could walk miles in those. My stomach growled, interrupting my fake-date planning, and I suddenly had a strong craving for something warm, creamy, and carb filled.

Grilled cheese is an art form. First, you melt pure Irish butter in a pan over medium-low heat. Then you add thick-cut sourdough bread, extra-sharp aged cheddar, and salted tomato slices, topping the sandwich with the other slice of bread. Heat the sandwich on low so it doesn't burn, but rather, caramelizes. For the soup, heirloom tomato bisque requires a sleeve of crackers after the grilled cheese sandwich is gone. It's a meal so hearty, filling, and comforting that I was almost in tears while I was eating it because I couldn't believe I'd been eating so rigidly that year. All the lost time from my favorite foods seemed like such a waste.

That night, freshly showered in my comfiest pajamas, I polished off a bowl of popcorn while reading my devotional Bible study. A timely lesson on living for the ways of the world. I'd been living, dieting, and suppressing my joys to win Dallas's attention all year for a disillusioned idea that I was only worthy of his affection if I was the kind of girl I thought he wanted. I wrote these feelings down in the side margins, and while I still didn't understand why, I knew I felt something when I looked at Dallas. He was incredibly good looking and had great muscular definition. While my initial attraction may have only been for his outward appearance, I hoped to get to know him more at that time since things were moving along.

The ruse with Tucker, though equally beneficial because it seemed I was already making progress with Dallas, made me incredibly nervous. I didn't like being dishonest but knowing why Tucker needed my help for his image, and after he assured me that night that he wasn't worried about missing out on anything else, I let it go for the night, feeling a little less worried, and I went to sleep.

The next morning, I dressed in the clothes I picked out the night before and took extra time doing my makeup, going so far as to add a little champagne-colored glimmer to my lids and a highlight to my cheekbones. Chocolate brown eyeliner made the slightest cat eye look, and a soft peachy bronzer gave my skin a subtle glow. It was certainly more of a "night" look, but I would have been going straight from work to the pumpkin patch with Tucker, so I didn't have time to do it later.

I arrived at work an hour early, as it was the day that Laney, Blair and I did each other's nails. It was our tradition since high school; each one of us would take turns getting our acrylic nails filled and painted while the other two did one hand at a time. It was how we discovered our love for the craft, and it certainly made it fun for us to all have special nails all the time and get to try out new products.

When I walked into the salon, Laney gave me a big smile. "Well, don't you look extra beautiful today! Big date tonight?" I didn't even have to look to know she was holding a pink cup, meaning Tucker told her we were going to the pumpkin patch that night. Sure enough, she lifted her cup and took a sip.

"You know it." I smiled back, giving my hair a playful flip. Then I noticed Blair looked a little down. "What's wrong, Blair?

"It's Cody. He's decided to leave for the mission, and he will be gone by next week, before the Pumpkin Stampede even kicks off. I'm going to miss him so much." Laney put her arm around Blair, giving her a kiss on the top of her head.

"Time goes by so fast, sis. He will be back before you know it," Laney consoled her sister.

"I know. I just really love him and selfishly want him all to myself. But he's out there doing the Lord's work, and I respect that, too. Just talking about it makes me feel God's comfort."

"That's so beautiful, Blair," I added. Her eyes perked up.

"I have an idea! Would you and Tucker like to go on a double date with us before Cody leaves? Otherwise, he won't get to meet Tucker until he gets back. In a year." Her eyes welled up and her chin trembled. I would do anything for either of those ladies, and I hated seeing Blair sad.

"Of course. Any night that works for you. I'm sure we could make it work." I looked out the front bay windows to see Tucker setting up a wooden sign outside of his truck with the day's specials, and my heart had a pang. I really hoped he wouldn't mind that I was setting him up for more dates with me.

"Great, Ginger! I'll text him right now. This will be good, because now he can put a face to the name as surely I'll be filling him in on every little detail of all of our lives for the next twelve months." The heart pang happened again, and that time, I recognized it. It was guilt. What was that all for, really? I thought about coming clean right then and there. But something deep inside of me didn't want to. Tucker was... A really great guy. If things started to show promise with Dallas, I would just have to create a reason for us to break up, though I struggled to find a reason that would justify such an action at the moment.

Our nails were well underway as we started with Laney's. She wanted her acrylics with pink tips, orange polka dots, and teal pumpkins scattered among them. I was next up, and I did a solid teal and hot pink combo on alternating nails. Blair, with a flair for nail decals, decided to add light turquoise pumpkin decals and little hearts and horseshoes to each nail. It was so cute and matched Laney's, so when Blair was up, she surprised us when she went with something entirely different.

"Can you do white French tips and no art?" Laney gasped at Blair's request.

"Blair, it's *autumn.* Our season of the pumpkin. What's going on here?" Laney questioned her sister, but Blair shook her head.

Ginger's Polished Thoughts

That saying about hearts being made to be broken? Except, its nails are made to be painted.

"I know. I just want this clean look for right now." She went quiet as she held her hands out delicately. We knew she was feeling very sad at the moment, so the words went unspoken as we did her French tip set. Her nails looked beautiful when we were done. She was just putting her hands under the UV light for the last time when our first clients walked in for the day.

"Hannah, Jolene. So nice to see you ladies." The mother and daughter duo took a seat at Laney's and my station while we started on their nails.

"Hannah is engaged!" Jolene excitedly spoke about her daughter, who was just a year or two out of high school. Hannah held up the back of her hand and we all reacted excitedly to her lovely, solitaire princess-cut ring.

"Oh, really? Who's the lucky guy?" As she told me the story of her high school sweetheart proposing in a field of late-season wildflowers last month, I realized how much I desired to be loved. I wanted to be a wife. I wanted a family one day. As I painted her nails with a glittery, opalescent finish, I daydreamed about what my life would be like when I was married. For some reason, I couldn't picture my husband.

Yes, I was head-over-heels for Dallas. But was he... *It?* I still wasn't sure, considering he hadn't been fully engaged in me yet, and it was a really odd feeling to analyze.

The day dragged on as our second, third, and fourth sets of clients came in. At one point, all three of us were doing Pumpkin Spice Pedicures at the same time. The fumes must have been really getting to us, because when our client Rachel walked in with a tray of baked goods from Tucker's truck, we all went ravenous.

"Just a little treat for my girls." Rachel had enough baked goods to feed us all for a week, and we thanked her profusely, taking a few bites before saving them until after our clients left. And the moment they did, we dug in like no one was watching.

"Ginger, I haven't seen you eat like this since last year," Laney whispered as I devoured a cinnamon maple sugar muffin.

"Can you really blame me, Laney? These are incredible." Laney just looked at me with a smile.

"I'm really happy, Ginger. Look at you, eating normally and crushing on a really nice guy. You're absolutely *glowing.*" I pulled back from Laney and turned to face a mirror that was above our hand-washing sink.

My face was looking the teeniest bit fuller since yesterday, no doubt from all the excess sugar and salt from last night's pie, savory dinner, and popcorn. But it rounded my face in a way that gave me a little plumpness to my cheekbones, and Laney was right. I did look healthier already.

"Thank you, Laney," I said.

"I don't have anyone else today, so I'm going to take a few treats to go. I'm off to see Cody," Blair smiled, seemingly a little more perked up than she was that morning. She had been on her phone with every second of down time she had that day. Her black hair looked sleek and shiny as usual, her makeup soft, and her dark rimmed glasses were off in favor of her contact lenses.

"You look great, Blair. Have fun," I said as she left, to which she gave us both a wave.

"It's too bad they will be apart for a year," I said with a sigh once she was gone. "They seem like the perfect match."

"I know it. But Blair is strong. If I know my sister, she's already decided he's the one for her. My hunch is they get married the same week he returns." We smiled at the thought.

"Yes, definitely. Blair's wedding will probably be really small and intimate. Just your folks, Bruce, me, and Cody's family. I don't see her doing anything else." I thought of what my life would be like in a year from then and wondered if I would be in a relationship. I said a silent prayer for my love life.

"Or maybe she will just elope." Laney's statement made us both chuckle and then look at each other.

"I could see it," I said.

"Me, too. We shall see what that girl does. For now, we just need to be keeping her busy and not wallowing in sadness. Maybe we could set up some girls' nights in advance. Even a little trip somewhere? She needs things to look forward to in the meantime," Laney said.

"I love that idea, Laney. We could go to a beach somewhere. Or the desert. Or Dollywood." My suggestions were long.

"Dollywood? Now you're talking! You know very well I have a pink sequined fringe jumpsuit I've been wanting to wear for years." Laney rubbed her hands together.

"Didn't you buy that to wear for your bachelorette party? I thought we were all going to dress up and go see the rodeo upstate. What happened to that plan?" I asked.

"Yes, I did. And I still want to do that sometime. Although living here does take the glamour away from traveling to see a rodeo because we are just mere *seconds* from the top rodeos in the world. But yeah, that plan was exciting until I realized in just a handful of hours we could be watching a real Broadway musical in Denver."

"I did love that rendition of *Cats,* " I said.
"Where were we?" I asked, looking at my watch. Laney pulled out her appointment book, taking another bite of her cinnamon maple scone.

"Oh, shoot. You're done for the day too, girlie." She smiled and winked, knowing full well I was off to the pumpkin patch.

"What about you? Can you manage the rest of today alone?" I asked.

"Yep, I just have Tasha coming in for a mani-pedi, *sans-Pumpkin Spice.* This poor soul doesn't like the scent, and she lives in Maple Haven. Can you imagine?" I shook my head and laughed, grabbing my purse from my station.

"Okay then, I'm off to the pumpkin patch."

"Have fun. I can't wait to hear about it tomorrow," Laney beamed, and I exited the salon as her next client, Tasha, was arriving.

Tucker was serving a few customers coffees when I walked up. I must have looked ready to go because he gave me a wave and looked like he was moving at high speeds. The scent of buttery sweetness was wafting on overload from his truck; it must have been the piles of pies he was taking out to the patch that smelled extra sweet.

Finally, the last customer was served. "Hey, Ginger. I'll be right out," Tucker said with a smile. As Tucker carried out several large brown paper bags from the back of his dessert truck, I waited beside it. He had at least ten pies he was transporting, and suddenly I realized we needed wheels to do so.

"Should I get my car?" I pointed to all the bags. He shook his head.

"Nope, I got my truck just right down the street. I can carry most of these if you don't mind carrying two? One in each hand?" I felt relieved as my car was sort of a mess inside with scarves, hats and jackets, since the weather there was so tumultuous all the time. I accepted the bags and was pleasantly surprised at how light they were.

"What's in these bags? It feels like almost nothing in them." I peeked inside, spotting a bright pink box with a twine bow. Tucker's bags, on the other hand, looked like they were about to give out from the weight, but he carried them effortlessly.

"Those are tonight's samples for you to try. I didn't want them to get lost in the shuffle." Tucker winked at me, and I felt my cheeks redden. He was really sweet.

Just a block down the road was a beautifully restored robin's egg blue vintage pickup truck. "Wow! Look at that truck." I pointed to it, marveling at its shiny, silver fixtures and wood paneling on the pickup bed.

"I'm glad you like it," Tucker said, as my jaw dropped.

"It's yours?" He took a few steps ahead and put the paper bags in the back of the truck.

"Yep. I restored it all through high school and college with my dad. It was our little weekend project for years. It's mostly modern under the hood, with the exception of air conditioning." He looked at me with a sheepish smile.

"Well, it's cold for most of the year here. The heat usually drops off like a rock after mid-July, and it's very pleasant out until the end of summer. This year has actually been a bit warmer than usual." I said it as if he was staying, which I remembered it was still up in the air if he was. "If you stay here, I mean. It wouldn't be so bad to go without air conditioning in this part of the Rockies." Tucker smiled.

"I'll keep that in mind," he said, coyly. We got in the truck, and I ran my fingers along the beautiful, white upholstery inside. The leather was stitched with thread that matched the paint color. A white steering wheel and a shiny, silver dash gave way to all the beautiful retro knobs and buttons. It was a gorgeous vehicle; one that you would have seen in a photoshoot full of pumpkins. The truck started with a purr, and we smoothly drove away.

"Now, off to the pumpkins," Tucker said. "The owner ordered a dozen pies to serve at a gathering they are hosting. I'm really thankful for the order, though it was a little difficult to manage in my food truck. But it led to some other connections because The Pumpkin Perk Cafe let me come in last night and use their kitchen."

"Wow! That's perfect. Maybe that can turn into something more?" I said, cheerfully.

"I hope it does. I really do like it here in Maple Haven so far." A slight tension was felt between us. "Anyway, you are welcome to eat your samples now or later. You can even take them home, just as long as you tell me what you think of them." My mouth watered at the thought.

"I ate several of your treats today as it was," I laughed, feeling the sugar high still. "Our client Rachel brought them in." Tucker smiled and nodded.

"Yes, Rachel. I met her at church last weekend. She's a nice girl." Suddenly, I felt a little twinge of... jealousy. I said a silent prayer for my feelings. Rachel was a stunning brunette with big, brown eyes and dark lashes. She had tanned skin and gentle freckles along her cheeks. She was a few years older than me, and I didn't know her well, except that she was incredibly kind.

"What church did you go to?" I asked, wanting to change the subject.

"Whispering Pines Church." Ahh, I thought. So, we have that in common.

"Good choice. I go there myself, and I love it." They had the best worship music around, plus, Blair was dating Cody, who ministered there.

"I really connected with the pastor. Cody? He's really got a way of making connections to our day-to-day lives from the ancient biblical stories. Wow."

"He really does. You know Blair from my salon? They are dating. He's actually about to leave on a year-long mission trip next week, right before the Pumpkin Stampede starts." Tucker nodded.

"Cody mentioned that he might be leaving. That's unfortunate for us, but the people he will help are so lucky to have a guy like him there. I didn't realize he was with Blair. From the minor interactions I've had with both of them face-to-face, I imagine they would make a really nice couple." We chatted about the church the rest of the short drive, eventually pulling up into a parking spot marked by a hay bale.

A large sign with chipped paint read, "Welcome to the Maple Haven Pumpkin Patch." There was a sprawling corn maze, a small petting zoo with colorful goats, and a small farm to table restaurant that served homemade cider and lemonade refreshers, along with a selection of savory foods. Their most infamous concoction was a grilled sunflower head. Tucker jumped out and grabbed the bags of pies, taking all of them in one trip.

"I'll be right back. I'm just going to drop these off at the front. Want to help me find some pie pumpkins when I'm done?" Tucker asked.

"Sure. Shall I meet you at the little barn over there?" I pointed to the hayride area.

"Okay. Be back in a flash." I watched Tucker walk effortlessly while carrying the heavy bags of pies. I hadn't noticed before just how broad his shoulders were. I closed my eyes and shook out the thought from my mind; Tucker and his gorgeous curly haired head were starting to get under my skin. I needed to stay focused and remember I was there with him to get Dallas's attention. Ah, yes, Dallas: The quiet, moody gym bro that I found attractive. Sure, I couldn't tell if there was truly anything more to him than training ponies, but he sure did look good while doing it.

Tucker returned before I knew it, empty handed and with a full smile. "They loved the pie, and they want to sell my slices here all season long." He was beaming with joy.

"That's excellent, Tucker. This really is your gift, you know! We have never had a baker as good as you in Maple Haven. Like, ever. Not even close."

"They said something similar inside. I'm just honored. All glory to God; I couldn't have done any of this without Him. And I feel like He is leading me down a very exciting new adventure." Tucker was giddy, and his energy was contagious. It was only a few minutes later until I felt like I was bouncing off the walls, too.

As we waltzed over to the pumpkins, I had forgotten how large the patch was. "They really make you work for the pumpkins here, don't they?" I asked Tucker as I scanned the daunting acreage.

"There—see? Pie pumpkins. Shouldn't there be a hayride somewhere around here to shuttle us there?" I scoured the fields and saw the transportation on the polar opposite end.

"It might be a while." I gestured to the truck. Tucker shrugged.

"I'm fine with walking. I wouldn't mind getting some more steps in," he said. So, we made our way to the pie pumpkins, conversing about everything under the sun on the way over. I couldn't help but enjoy how natural things felt between us. We were meant to be friends, I decided. When we finally arrived at the right place, I spotted a perfectly-plump, evenly-round white whale of a pie pumpkin.

"Look how perfectly proportioned this one is!" I ran over to it, sitting down next to it as I lifted it in my lap. It was still attached to the vine, which is another thing I realized I'd forgotten: That farm was a U-Pick style.

"Wow, it really is a good one. Nice job, Ginger." Tucker had his hands in his pockets, perfectly content to let me pick out the pumpkins, which I was enjoying. I found a few more, and we started marking them with a small bottle of pink nail polish that I had in my purse, putting a tiny dot of polish on each stem that we needed to cut. When we were done, there were five pumpkins total that we were going to get. Next, was to figure out how to get them untethered from the very thick and spiny vines.

"I think I can just pull it with all my might and break it." Tucker watched me as I went in with total confidence.

"Are you sure? That's kind of an awkward pull. You don't want to hurt your back." Before he was done warning me of injury, I was already bent over in a full-blown tug of the heaviest pie pumpkin known to man. As I pulled up, it gave a little slack and went back down fast. I caught myself from doing a complete somersault with the pumpkin in tow by straightening my back. On my second attempt, I got down on my knees and lifted with the strength of my legs and arms at once. It was much more promising, until the pumpkin vine suddenly broke without warning and I fell backwards, landing in a pile of imperfectly placed hay.

"I did it!" I yelled out, rolling the pumpkin off of me while Tucker laughed hysterically. I stood back up, which made him chuckle even harder. "What is it?" I shrugged, and he walked over to me and pulled out large clumps of hay from my hair.

"That was cute. I had no idea you had so much *spunk.*" I wasn't sure how to react to him calling me *cute,* nor to the fact that I *liked it.* But for now, I would just focus on the fact that I was already dressed like a scarecrow—I didn't need the hay in my hair to complete the ensemble.

Small Town Wisdom

Scarecrows are just men who were turned to bags of hay after hearing the gossip coming out of the nail salon.

The truck pulling the hayride trailer around reached us on its rounds shortly after my stunt with the hay. A small family was in the back of it, sitting on bales when the man jumped out and offered his pocketknife to cut the rest of the pumpkin stems, to which we agreed. After the three of us quickly loaded them into the back of the trailer, the truck started up again, and we went on a scenic route through the rest of the patch.

Space was limited in the back trailer, and Tucker and I were pressed together like bread. We were still giggling about the evening, and I kept catching a whiff of vanilla, cinnamon and a leathery musk before I realized it was Tucker. Some men smelled like aftershave; he smelled like dessert and masculinity. As the night came to a close, and we passed several families picking out their perfect porch pumpkins, something came over me. A calmness, a joy that I wasn't familiar with. Tucker must have felt the same because he quietly put his hand over mine, which rested on my lower thigh. I turned my hand quickly, *too quickly,* and just like that, we were holding hands. I was immediately reminded that this wasn't a relationship—rather an arrangement—but boy, did it feel nice to have the attention from Tucker. I didn't know what it meant, but right then, I didn't care. It was nice.

CHAPTER 6:
CINNAMON, COWBOYS & CHEMISTRY

The next morning at the salon, I relished to Laney and Blair about my time with Tucker at the pumpkin patch, telling them everything.

"And then when we got back to the truck, I sampled his latest creation: *brown sugar pumpkin cheesecake.* Ladies—it was beyond anything I've ever tasted in my life. It had a caramelized top crust! I ate the whole slice, and he certainly didn't skimp this time." My laughter filled the room as I recalled every moment, to which the sisters lapped up, sharing my joy.

"That sounds heavenly! Do you think he has any left over? I'd like to get in on this sampling situation." Laney stood with a wink, shaking her coffee cup and signaling to Blair that she was empty. "Does anyone need another?"

Blair shook her head. "I'm going to need to pull out the pants I reserve for Thanksgiving dinner if I have any more treats this week." Laney and Blair had always been slender and always on the go. I was sure the two things correlated, and they had nothing to worry about in the waistline department.

"Now, how are things with Cody?" I turned the conversation over to Blair.

"So great. That man is a Godsend. He is taking me out tonight again. Actually," Blair looked inquisitive, "do you and Tucker want to join? We are going to that cute retro diner off highway 440. You know the one? The *Harvest Moon Cafe.*"

"In all my life, I've never actually been there, but I've always wanted to go." I smiled at Blair in excitement. "I'll ask Tucker if he's free."

"In that case, will you get my refill for me? It's the Caramel Chai." Laney made a heart with her hands and winked at me as her first client of the day walked in. Blair's client had been running late, and I didn't have anyone for another half hour, so I agreed to go.

"Good morning, Tucker," I said, completely perked up to the sky with happiness that morning. I didn't even know why I felt so great, but I attributed it to consuming extra sugar. It did wonders for my mood, even if my waistline was starting to feel a little fuller. Tucker's hair looked curlier than usual under his cowboy hat as he turned around to greet me.

"Hi, Ginger," he beamed, the amber flecks in his eyes lighting up like a candle inside of a pumpkin. "I made this for you." He slid a cup over to me, and I no longer felt the need to quiz him of its contents before taking a sip. Flavors of caramel decadence hit all of my senses, along with an undertone of oat milk.

"That is so good; thank you. Just what I needed," I smiled, taking another generous swig. "Blair, Cody's girlfriend? She invited you and me out to the *Harvest Moon Cafe* tonight. If you'd like to go, anyway. I realize this isn't really part of our plan, so..." Tucker's expression changed, and it looked like he was deep in thought.

"Sure. I would like to see Cody," Tucker said plainly.

"Ok, great!" We just stood there for a moment in silence. "Oh, Laney would like another Caramel Chai as well." I laid out her money, plus I put another few dollars in his tip jar. He gave me a look.

"You don't have to tip me, Ginger. That coffee was a gift." Suddenly, I felt awkward in my own skin.

"I know it was, and I thank you. But I would *also* like to be generous." Tucker nodded, not saying much else.

"I am almost done making a fresh batch of Caramel. It just needs to simmer for a little bit. Could I bring the coffee to Laney in a few minutes? I used the last of what I had on your coffee." It was then when I noticed he seemed a little... off that morning.

"Oh, of course. Laney can wait. Take your time." Tucker nodded and turned back around. I stood there for a moment, before accepting the conversation was over, and went back to the salon. What in the world was that?

As I traipsed back inside, I told Laney he was bringing it by, and she nodded, not interrupting her client telling her a story about a date she just went on. It sounded either really bad, or really amazing, because all I kept hearing from Laney was "wow," as she filed her client's nails.

Blair's client showed while I was gone, and she had just started an amber vanilla pedicure with a cinnamon foot scrub. I still had more time to kill, but I felt anxious about Tucker. Had something gone wrong last night, and I didn't see it? Had he changed his mind about our exchange? He did agree to go to the dinner that night, so at least that was a win.

I decided to sit in the massage chair at an empty pedicure booth while I passed the time but found myself being a little too obvious about waiting. So, I pulled out my phone and began an endless doom scroll.

When the door opened again, I looked up with a huge smile. But it wasn't Tucker—it was *Dallas.* Everyone in the salon perked up. What in the world was this?

"Hello," Laney said, giving me a look of confusion since I was still sitting and hadn't greeted him or figured out why he was there.

"Hi," Dallas said to her, then turned his eyes to me. I stood up, robotically getting out of the chair.

"Hi, Dallas." I walked over to him, not knowing what else I should do. You could hear a pin drop in the salon. The girls stopped their scrubbing and filing, and I thought the music even paused itself so it could listen in.

"I was wondering if you could look at my foot," Dallas hammered out, looking like a fish out of water, and maybe feeling like one, too. He looked around the salon at all the women looking at him.

"He wants you to look at his foot, Ginger," Blair whispered, as I stood there still in shock. I don't know what was wrong with me, but something about seeing him in my place of business was very strange.

"Yes, yes, of course. I, uh, have an appointment in about fifteen minutes, but I do have a few minutes before that, if you, uh, want to have a seat." I couldn't stop rambling as I motioned to the seat I was just lounging in, and he slipped off his tennis shoe and sock, putting it up on the bowl. I pulled my short chair over and put gloves on, and then I took a glance. I gasped out loud. Dallas had some serious foot *problems* that I wasn't sure I could help with, even if I had a PhD. "You need to see a doctor, Dallas. This looks beyond what I can assist with, unfortunately. It looks like the nail is hanging on by a thread." His poor toe was inflamed to the point I didn't know why he wasn't in an emergency room right then.

"Oh, okay. Thanks for looking," he smiled and put his sock and shoe back on, while I cleaned up the station again before removing the gloves and washing my hands.

"I'm sorry I couldn't help. I'd seek medical care as soon as possible. That doesn't look good." I put my hands in my back pockets as he lingered.

"So, I was thinking."

I could hear Laney in the background clear her throat, knowing exactly what she would say at that moment if she could: "*He was thinking, Ginger!*"

"Yeah?" I asked. I wasn't even sure where that was going.

"We are having a Fall party at *Maple Muscle Gym.* Do you want to come? It's tonight." My heart sank. I had already made plans that night with Blair, Cody and Tucker. I thought of all the ways I could sneak out of it before feeling horrible guilt because Cody was leaving and so I decided against it.

"I have plans tonight, actually." I looked over at Blair, to see if she was listening in. She was.

"Well, that's okay. I'll see you soon for a session?" Why did he make it sound like a date?

"Yes, I would like that." The vibe in the salon shifted, and I heard Laney clear her throat again. I knew I'd just ticked someone off.

"Okay, then. See you later." Dallas left the salon, and I turned to walk back to where I was sitting, like nothing happened, knowing the girls would jump right in and give their two cents whether good or bad. They never held back, and despite how I acted when they did, I loved them for it. But neither Laney nor Blair said anything to me. In fact, no one said a word to me. It was like I was invisible. A moment later, Tucker came with Laney's coffee. I was overtly aware that it would have been impossible for him to not pass Dallas on his way in.

"Hi, Tucker." Laney stood, and Tucker also looked right past me. "Thank you, sir." She held it up and motioned her appreciation. Finally, after what felt like a very lonely minute, Tucker turned to me and pulled out the book in his shirt pocket.

"I wanted to give you this last night, but I forgot." Between the pages he pulled out a beautiful three-colored, perfect leaf. It started with yellow at the top and blended into orange and red. It looked like fire, and it smelled like his scent of musky cinnamon and vanilla, I could tell, even just from holding it at a distance. I wanted to fill the silence with a comment about Dallas, feeling like it was impertinent that I explain myself, but it was neither the time nor place. And even if it was, we had an agreement.

"It's beautiful. Thank you." He cracked a smile, but it didn't reach his eyes, and he walked out without another word.

With him leaving, my client walked in, and I wondered what all of it meant, and where my loyalty would lay. I was aware the second our clients left, Laney was going to lay into me, as she was always the first to hold me accountable. I could almost feel her words forming in her mind as she sat a few chairs down from me.

"What kind of food do you think they serve at a party inside of a *gym,* anyway?" Laney asked rhetorically to the room of ladies.

Favorite Fall Recipes (after blowing your diet)
Chocolate syrup

A few laughs were let out, including from me, as my client, Stella, took a seat. Stella was sweet sixteen and got manicures every two weeks. She had beautiful nail beds and took meticulous care of her appearance. From the outside looking in, she was flawless with her soft, olive skin and freckles. She had naturally dark red hair and all around was a stunning beauty.

"Hi, Stella. What are we doing today?" Stella whipped out her phone to show me a photo of watercolor painted nails in warm, autumn hues. "That will look gorgeous on you, girl. Let's do it." I started with removing her current polish, cleaning up her cuticles, and buffing away any minor imperfections, and since I desperately needed to get my mind off Tucker and Dallas, I tried to get Stella to talk more.

"So, how's school? Any fun things happening? Are you going to the homecoming dance?" I peppered off questions so I could focus on the task and listen as I worked on her nails. She was quieter than usual but eventually started.

"School is okay, I just can't wait to be done. Two more years." Stella let out a long sigh." *Uh oh, I thought.* "And I haven't been asked to the dance yet, despite. . ." She trailed off. I could feel her sadness as if it were my own.

"Despite what, Stella?" I asked quietly. She paused, finally offering it up.

"Despite working out extra this summer. Doing tennis. Running indoor track. I've been working so hard to be toned and fit so that I can fit in." Stella was an active teenager, whose story sounded very familiar.

"Stella- I think it's great you're so athletic. But is it for the right reasons? Why do you feel you need to do this?" I put the file down, hoping to connect with her sadness.

"I just want to feel pretty... And be noticed." That hit me hard. I related so much to this girl as I reflected on my own journey of seeking Dallas's attention. I'd be a hypocrite if I told her anything but the truth about my own walk down the same road, so I did.

"I know just what you're experiencing, Stella. I've been doing the same thing all year to gain the attention of a guy." Stella's eyes brightened, and her lips turned up in a smile.

"And? Is it working?" I shrugged my shoulders.
"Not really, no. I mean, maybe now that I've actually been eating what I want again, including lots of dessert—he's sort of coming around. In fact, he just came in here a little while ago to ask me out. Funny how that works." Stella nodded, looking down at her nails. I looked over her shoulder and saw Tucker handing a

pink bag to a customer. I hated admitting it to myself, but it was time. "But the right man? He's going to want you to eat, to be healthy and strong. He will never want you to be skipping meals or torturing yourself for attention." Stella shrugged, eventually nodding.

"Yeah, I figured. It's just that the girls at my school are all so perfect. They play all the sports and are good at everything. I just want to fit in," Stella spoke softly.

"You are perfect, too. Here, I have an idea." I put down the bottle of gel base coat and pulled out a small notepad that I had bought for tracking my calories. I tore out the three pages I filled with my miserly calorie counts before switching to a calorie-counting app and handed it to her. "Why don't you write something down every day that makes you feel beautiful? And Stella, I know it doesn't seem like it now, but your worth is not in the eyes of another. It's in the eyes of God alone." She took the notepad and smiled.

"Thanks, Ginger. I'll try it out. Do you do this, too?" Her question pained me even more, but I had to be honest with her once again.

"No, but I need to. I'm a total hypocrite, Stella. I just don't want you to make the same mistakes I have and be chasing the wrong goals in life." Wait—did I just say that—the *wrong* goals?

Sure, Dallas wasn't perfect, but my approach to the whole scenario was one that reeked of boredom and the dreaded *desperation.* No wonder he was starting to come around since I had my eye on someone else. Or, at least, pretended to.

"Thank you for sharing that, Ginger." Stella was chattier the rest of our appointment, as I encouraged her to consider going to homecoming with friends instead of relying on a date.

"I remember my senior prom," I said, as Laney finished up her client and looked my way.

"Ah, prom. Wasn't that fun, just the three of us? Oh wait, I forgot. Ginger had to bring a date," Laney teased.

I elaborated to Stella. "Yep, that's right. I felt pretty glum about not getting asked, so when a friend of mine offered to take me, I accepted." Stella's eyes got wide.

"That's great! Then you didn't have to go alone," she added.

"Well, the thing was, everyone whom I wanted to dance with was there solo. Or *going stag,* as we say. Meanwhile, I felt chained to my date, who thought maybe this was a *real date,* which I had no intention of. It was all very *awkward.* My point is, had I just attended in style, I would have had the freedom to chat and dance with anyone I wanted. Waiting for an invitation to something that I didn't need one for kind of ruined the evening."

"And don't forget to tell Stella about his hairdo," Blair added, not even looking up from the long set of dip nails she was creating.

Ginger's Polished Thoughts
If only you could buff out life's regrets like a fresh set of acrylics.
On second thought, I'm pretty sure "buff out" is a term used by mobsters.

"I wouldn't call it a mullet, but it wasn't quite a mohawk either. It was a strange combination of something right in the middle." Stella giggled while our door chimed once more. It was _Tucker,_ and my heart sank. He was holding a platter of baked goods.

"Oh look, it's your man, Ginger!" Laney ran over to greet him.

Tucker didn't seem to react to Laney. "I'm closing up early today and I have some extras, if you ladies wanted anything? I can take them next door if—" Laney cut Tucker off.

"No, no. We can definitely _help you out._ We will take them off your hands." Laney grinned ear to ear at me while I just smiled.

"Will we see you tonight, Tucker?" Blair asked, finally looking up from her client's hands.

"Yes, I can make it. I just have something I need to do beforehand." I could tell that nosey Laney was dying to ask *what*, and it was killing her not to, but I honestly wished she would have already. Instead, a silent, awkward moment passed as Laney then nodded to Tucker and took the tray of delectable goods. "Ginger, shall I meet you there?"

"Sure. I think it's at six, right Blair?" I turned it to her but didn't take my eyes off Tucker who still seemed very *off.*

"Yes, six. See you then." Blair gave him a smile and continued her work as Tucker left the salon. The set of dip nails Blair was working on were bright blue, a reprieve from the fall colors that we were normally doing back-to-back. As I looked a little closer, I noticed her other hand was pink nails, and then I realized it was for a gender reveal as her client, Becky, was pregnant.

"Here, girls." Laney held out the tray to us, and I could see Stella's hesitation. It broke my heart. So, I decided to take the lead.

"Mmm... I'll take this one. And maybe another for later, so don't go eating them all, Laney." I grabbed a muffin with a crumble topping that smelled overwhelmingly of apple and brown sugar.

"Har, har," Laney quipped, motioning for Stella to make her selection. Stella paused, finally taking a cupcake with cream frosting and little orange sprinkles.

"Thank you," Stella said, setting the cupcake down at her side.

"You have to tell me what flavor that is," I said, before taking a generous bite of my own treat. Its texture was like a cloud, stuffed with baked apple chunks and a delightful creme filling. Tucker was going to be the death of my waistline. I put the muffin back down, and Stella finally took a small bite of hers. I could feel the energy in the room shift when she started chewing.

"Oh my," Stella whispered, nodding. "Yep, that's worth it." She took another bite—that time, a real one. "It's carrot cake with those golden raisins. I *love* raisins."

"I'll be sure to pass it along to the chef," I smiled.

"You mean, the *muffin man?*" Laney was heard giggling from the supply closet where I just knew she was snacking on our treat tray.

"Did all of that sugar go to your head or are you actually going to start calling him that?" Blair asked her sister.

"Maybe a little of both? You gotta admit, it's a catchy name," Laney grinned, holding a pumpkin scone. The two of them started singing the song of Tucker's new namesake, while I tried my best not to follow along, lest I accidentally call him that in person.

As I finished Stella's nails, I liked to think she left *The Cozy Cuticle* in a better place than when she came in. But I didn't know for sure. All I knew was that I needed to pray for her and re-evaluate my own priorities that suddenly looked very out of whack to reality. While there was nothing wrong with wanting to be healthy, the strictness of my lifestyle wasn't. It was okay to enjoy an indulgence now and then. I finished my muffin, considering that maybe then, I was approaching too many sugary indulgences, but that was neither here nor there.

Working on the nails of my last client of the day, Kendall, a thirty-something novelist who wrote crime fiction and notoriously over-analyzed my every move, I considered what it was that I liked about Dallas, and why I didn't feel the same towards Tucker. Filing away at Kendall's pink acrylic French tips, she interrupted my thoughts.

"So... I bet clients really get to talking when they sit in your chair." Kendall was speaking in a low tone. I shrugged and nodded.

"Yeah, sure. Especially because I spend an hour with them twice a month, it happens that I do get to know almost everyone," I used *almost* because other than Kendall's career, I knew very little about her. When I walked past the bookstore, *The Corner Nook,* sometimes I saw her books on display in the window. All of them usually had some variation of a weapon on the cover and a smiling couple. They were the types of books that followed couples where "you'd never see it coming" type of trope. Entertaining, but a little dark for my blood. Kendall looked deep in thought for a moment before continuing.

"Does anyone ever...confess to anything?" I tried to keep a straight face while I dipped my acrylic brush into the activator powder to apply to her nails, suddenly understanding where she was getting at. Kendall needed *material.* I decided to tell her just what I knew.

"Oh yes, all the time." I turned my voice into a low whisper, moving my head a little closer. "Once, a client told me that she bought pre-made deli salads and presented them as her own at the church potluck."

Kendall lost interest in our conversation and pulled out her e-reader, and I let my mind go back to Tucker, remembering the pact we made. Him adding in, "No falling in love." What did that mean? And who was it intended for?

*****

Arriving at the *Harvest Moon Cafe*, I pulled into a parking spot front and center. The air was chilly, and the wind was howling. While I enjoyed autumn evenings, it felt like there was a windstorm rolling in. Putting on a cozy shacket, that was really just a thicker plaid shirt that wore like a jacket, I stepped out of my car and walked inside. Blair and Cody were already looking cozy in a retro-style booth, while Tucker was nowhere to be seen. My heart sank thinking he didn't show, but I wasn't sure it was because I wanted to see him, or I'd hurt my friend for having to confess.

"Ginger! Over here," Blair hollered at me while I waited at the door, pretending to check my messages rather than face the music. I walked over, after having exactly zero new messages from Tucker, and sat opposite of the happy couple in the booth. "Thanks for coming, Ginger," Cody said softly. He had his arm around Blair.

"Thanks for having me. I guess Tucker hasn't shown yet?" My voice felt creaky.

"No, he's here. He was here when we arrived. There's just a gal he was talking to over there." Before Cody could even finish, I turned my head to see the top of Tucker's curls in another booth.

Who is he speaking with, I wondered? Should I be cool and patiently wait, or go over and see if he'll be joining us tonight?

"I think you should go get him, Ginger." Blair, always a mind reader and sensitive to my feelings, could tell I was feeling awkward about Tucker being over there. But the constant reminder that he wasn't actually dating me rang off in my head like an alarm bell: What Tucker did was none of my business.

"Nah, I think I'll just wait," I said, looking over the menu casually. Their selection of salads was surprisingly good; it wasn't another greasy diner after all. I was narrowing down my selections between the Harvest Pear Salad and the Arugula Crunch Salad when Tucker finally came over.

"Did you hear that *High Noon Horses* will be donating all of the proceeds from their trail rides this weekend to our church?" Cody asked us.

"That's great news! Maybe we should go. I haven't been on a horse in ages," Blair mumbled as she read the menu.

"I'm sorry for holding everyone up. I met a friend here earlier and lost track of time." I quickly looked over my shoulder to see just who the friend was, and I clenched my jaw as tight as it could go to keep it from opening wide. It was Samantha, the woman who was scowling at me from the nail salon. What on earth were they discussing? And why was I, once again, feeling... jealous?

"No worries," I said, looking back at the menu and pretending to be completely unbothered, when in fact, my mind was wrestling with just how *bothered* it was. Tucker slid into the booth next to me and picked up a menu.

"I think I'm going to get the chicken sandwich," Blair said to Cody, and in reading its description, my stomach growled. It sounded much more satiating than a salad.

"I'll get the same," I said to Blair, who smiled at me.

"Yay! Salad-only Ginger is gone." Blair and I chuckled while Tucker and Cody discussed their preference on cooking meat.

When the waitress arrived, she was a beautiful brunette woman about my age. I couldn't help but look to see if Tucker noticed her. *Ugh.*

"What can I get everyone?" Her name tag read *Mandy,* her bright pink lips matched her nails, and her perfect teeth were almost blinding with whiteness. She sat four waters on the table.

We all placed our orders, and Tucker was the last one to go. She stepped a little closer when it was his turn. "I think I'll get the French dip," Tucker spoke, not looking up from the menu. You could tell she was waiting for him to, as she took her time writing down his order.

"What else can I get you?" she asked. Tucker finally looked up. Mandy smiled and put a hand on her hip while she looked at him expectantly.

"How about fries?" She laughed as Tucker said that, though nothing about it was funny. Clearly, she was flirting with him. I took a deep breath and said a silent prayer for my ridiculous behavior. Why was this bothering me? I had no claim on him. As Mandy jotted down "fries," she gave a little wink and went on her way. I pretended not to notice, but Blair kicked my leg under the table. She saw the whole exchange. Perhaps the only one who didn't seem to react was Tucker, who remained neutral the entire time.

"So," Cody said, squeezing Blair a little tighter around her shoulder. "We have an announcement." They looked at each other lovingly for a moment before turning back to us. "We are getting married." A soft tear fell from Blair's eye, and she wiped it away. I'd never seen her happier.

"That's wonderful news! Congratulations to you both. I couldn't have picked a partner for either of you." I reached over the table and squeezed Blair's hand. On her ring finger was a lovely, delicate, diamond solitaire ring. "So, we will have much wedding planning to do while Cody's gone?" I smiled at Blair, knowing this would be a great thing for her to keep her busy for the twelve-month term. She shrugged a little and nodded.

"Yes, for sure." Her response was iffy, but I didn't think anything of it, as my mind was back on my own love life. Seeing Blair and Cody happily betrothed made me wish I was closer to that.

"Will you be at church on Sunday, Ginger?" Cody asked, bringing me out of my daydreams.

"Yes, definitely. I signed up to help out for the church's Fall Festival committee, too," I said.

"Well, in that case, Tucker, will you join Ginger for the committee? I think we can use all the help we can get. If you're available, that is," Cody asked.

Tucker nodded. "Sure. May I ask, what is the committee responsible for doing?"

"The church actually hosts several booths for the event. Like a 'guess how many candy corns in a jar' or scarecrow face painting. One year, we did a photo booth. We have most of our tables and materials ready to go. It's just going to require making fresh signs, entry forms, things like that."

"Sounds simple enough; I can help out. I'm available all-day Sunday. Saturday is going to be a little tight, I'm afraid."

"Oh yeah? Got plans, do you?" After the words came out of my mouth, I realized it sounded like I was talking in riddles.

"Yes. I have a big order I need to bake. It seems like everyone in this town is hosting a fall-themed party, among other things." Tucker smiled and sipped his water. "For once in my life, it appears I'm in the right place at the right time," he grinned.

"Congrats, Tucker. I think it's great that you're here in Maple Haven." Cody beamed at him. "I think I heard that you were pretty involved in rodeo before this—is that right?" Cody's inquiry was welcomed as I, too, wanted to hear more about his past.

Tucker nodded, taking another sip from his water. "Yep. I got into bronc riding at fifteen, much to my parents' dismay." He trailed off, reminiscing on the subject. "They always used to warn me I was going to get hurt. But what teenager listens to their parents? I made it pretty far, though: all the way to NFR in Vegas before a freak accident broke my back in three places." My eyes widened as he spoke. I knew Tucker said that his career ended at the NFR, but I assumed it was due to the implications of calling that woman out; I had no idea it was due to an injury. He continued. "It was when I was laid up in that hospital over Christmas that I asked God for a new path in life. That same day, my family surprised me by flying in for the holiday so we could spend it together, and my sister revealed she had just spent her life savings on a food truck and asked me if I would run it with her when I recovered. I didn't know it then, but she had stage 3 breast cancer and hadn't told us yet. My sister was like that. She loved all of us as hard as she could and never put herself first. I do wish she had shared her diagnosis with us sooner, though I understand why she didn't. She wasn't looking for sympathy, but rather, wanted to share as much of God's love as she could, while she could. When she passed, I found out the truck was registered in my name from day one. I took it as a good sign as any that God wanted me to give this a shot. So, here I am." I was floored by Tucker's story. Though he had shared with me mere pieces, I didn't know the whole of it.

"Thank you for sharing that, Tucker." I put my hand on top of his as it rested on the table. He looked over to me and was about to say something when the annoyingly gorgeous waitress returned. A frown was on her perfectly pink pout when she saw my hand on his. I quickly moved my hand as she started to set plates down, and her flirtatious personality returned instantly.

"Here ya go, handsome," she boldly spoke to Tucker, causing us all to shift a little in our seats. Tucker didn't say a word or look in her direction. "Can I get y'all anything else?" she asked, her hand on her hip popping out expectantly.

"I think we're good here," Cody said, as Blair handed me the ketchup after she put a generous amount down for her tater tots. I peeked over at Mandy, who smiled at me while she spun around on her heels. Tucker was extremely handsome, and while her behavior was more forward than most, was I really that surprised?

We ate our meal, idly chatting about life in Maple Haven and the upcoming fall festivities in town.

Small Town Wisdom

If you want to increase your attractiveness to a man who just ordered French fries, yield a bottle of ranch from your purse.

If you're not already carrying around a purse bottle of ranch dressing, are you even trying to catch a man?

The conversation shifted to Cody's upcoming trip. He was leaving in just a few short days and would be missing the Pumpkin Stampede, as he spoke fondly about his favorite events.

"You know, back in the day, I was asked to be the bachelor for the cowboy bachelor auction." He put his arm around Blair, giving her a squeeze while she giggled.

"Really? You never told me that!" He leaned in and kissed her forehead.

"Yes, ma'am. But don't worry. I wasn't cowboy enough in the end, and they didn't think the stick horse I brought was funny. They chose my cousin, Bobby, who actually knew how to ride a horse." We all chuckled.

"I'm okay with you not being cowboy enough. I love you just the way you are, Cody." They looked into each other's eyes for a moment while Tucker and I instinctively looked away, letting them share their moment.

"Speaking of the cowboy auction," Tucker spoke in a low voice, "I have been asked to be one of the cowboys up for charity. Sounds like a really good cause, actually, with all that money going to people in need locally." My heart sank. Of course, they would ask Tucker to be auctioned off for a date; I wasn't surprised, just aware of how ridiculously jealous I was feeling that night. Before I could hear another word, I excused myself from the table, letting Tucker slide out of the booth.

"I'll be right back; just need to go to the ladies room." As I treaded to the loo, my mind went haywire. Thankfully, I was alone in the bathroom when I opened the door. I walked to the sink, analyzing my reflection in the mirror. "Lord, I don't know where all of these feelings are coming from, but I know they are not from you. Please help me, Lord." Just then, Mandy waltzed in. We made an electrifying eye contact before she stopped at the mirror right next to me and reached in her apron, retrieving her tube of bright pink lipstick. As she reapplied, I started washing my hands for image sake.

"So, is that your boyfriend? He's pretty cute." Her lipstick was already pretty thick, and I felt like she had come in just to ask me that question. As I took the paper towels to wipe my hands, I was taken aback by the brazenness of this waitress who saw Tucker and me, in all appearances, on a date. And yet she still asked? It was like she could see right through me, and I didn't like it. I shrugged off her question and left without a word.

Back at the table, Cody was in the middle of a wild retelling of last year's bachelor auction. It looked like I was still going to hear all the details, and I remembered my prayer for the misplaced jealousy I was feeling.

"Then, good ole' Barry Quinn took the stage. He's a little more on the portly side, but just as eligible for a bachelor as any." Cody was very animated in his retelling. Tucker stood when he saw me, letting me slide back into the booth next to him.

"Barry owns that huge ranch out on Skull River, right? I can't remember the name," Blair looked at me, as if I would know.

"Oh, it's the, umm. . . *Crazy River Ranch*," Cody interjected. We all nodded in agreement. "So, as he took the stage, it looked like he went all out for a new outfit, but maybe the shirt didn't fit right as it was unbuttoned—all the way—and the sleeves were cut off! But that guy had the most heated bidding war I've ever seen! Women from all over the county wanted to be the woman to take him out on a date," Cody smiled.

"Or the wife of the man who owns that ranch." Tucker said what we were all thinking out loud.

"You know it!" Blair said, and I laughed.

"So, Tucker. What have you decided to volunteer for the cowboy bachelor auction, then?" Blair asked, while taking a bite of her tater tots. I shot her a glance, thanking her with my eyes for asking so I didn't have to.

"I'm not sure yet. It is the day after the pumpkin pie bake-off, so all of that would be behind me. What do you think I should do, Ginger?" He turned to me, putting me on the spot. The pumpkin pie bake-off was officially the end of our arrangement, and we both knew it. Was Tucker asking me this to see if I wanted to continue it or was I just over-analyzing things again?

I had two options there: I could have said he shouldn't do it, staking my claim on him, though I was still trying to pursue Dallas; or, I could have encouraged him to do it. It was for charity, after all. But I didn't do either of those things. Instead, I floundered.

"Oh, um, I don't know. Do you want to do it?" While I bombed my chance of having an opinion on the matter, my curiosity was heightened on if he wanted to do it or not. At that point, I was enjoying hanging out with Tucker, but my eye was still focused on Dallas.

"I don't know. It seems rather silly to me." He turned to look at me head on and gave me a devious smile. Something in his look told me he dared me to tell him not to do it. Which had the opposite effect.

"It *is* for such a good cause, though. Right? What are we funding this year?" I asked the group to see if anyone knew. Blair shrugged and looked at Cody.

"I think this year is benefiting the food pantry," Cody recalled.

"Oh! Yes, I heard about that! Aren't they getting a new addition put on to stock pet food, too?" Blair clutched her chest, moved by the charity.

"It's settled, then. I think you should do it, Tucker. There are so many people in our community who rely on the food pantry. I can't think of anything more important at this time." I felt convicted in my words, as I looked over to Tucker, and he nodded nonchalantly.

"I agree with that. Alright, as long as none of y'all have any objections..." Tucker gave me a sheepish look, but I didn't react. If it was *real*, I probably would've had a say in the matter. Right? Or would I have seen it for what it was: a charity benefiting from Tucker's good looks and cowboy image? There was just the one little, tiny fact that he would be going on a date with the winner, but for all I knew, Mrs. Haverly could've won, and I would have had nothing to worry about. If it *were* real, of course.

Blair and Cody looked at me expectantly, while I shook my head. "No, I think it's great, Tucker. I actually look *forward* to you being up for sale at the cowboy auction."

"Did I hear someone is gonna be up for sale?" Mandy, the waitress, came out of nowhere over to us and had her hand with its bright pink nails tapping the table. *Hmm. Dip nails. I wonder where she gets them done? There is only one other nail place in Maple Haven.* I snapped out of it and heard Tucker telling her he was going to be at the cowboy bachelor auction, to which Mandy let out a squeal. "That's just great. I look forward to buying a ticket or two." She gave him a wink and dropped the check on the table. "Check out right over there with Suzy when y'all are ready to get boot scootin' out of here." I thought it was over when she leaned over and whispered into Tucker's ear, before vanishing again to the back of the diner.

"What in the world did she say?" My eyes were huge as I looked at him; it wasn't lost on me that I had no problem with Tucker going up for auction, but something about that gorgeous waitress brazenly hitting on him threw me over the edge.

"Somethin' about her getting off work in an hour. Don't worry, darlin'. She's not my type." Tucker winked at me, and I felt the shock waning from my face.

"Gorgeous isn't your type?" I cocked an eyebrow at him.

"Nah. It's got nothing to do with looks." He looked straight ahead, but something in his tone made me believe him.

"Shall we get out of here? The mini golf place is still open one more hour." Cody proposed the idea, and while the weather was feeling chilly and blustery, I couldn't think of anything that sounded more fun to do with my best friend Blair, her new fiancé, and Tucker.

CHAPTER 7:

A CHILL IN THE BREEZE, A FLUTTER IN MY HEART

I rose early for my day off, starting it deep in prayer. I spent nearly an hour telling God about my feelings for Dallas, the situation with Tucker, and my thankfulness for my life. After much conversation and reflection, and with the Pumpkin Stampede only two days away, I felt convicted to stop playing games. The first thing I did was call the Maple Muscle Gym and cancel my training session for the day. For one, I was way too sore still from the last session. And two, I needed time to reflect. I would rather save my last session for when my mind was clearer on the subject than go in when I didn't know what I was feeling.

"Maple Muscle Gym, how can I help you?" Megan answered the phone in her usual perky voice.

"Hi Megan, this is Ginger. I have a session with Dallas this morning, and I'm sorry, but I need to cancel."

"That's so funny you called, Ginger. We were just about to call you and cancel," Megan laughed. "They are repaving our parking lot this morning. I had to walk from three blocks down just to man the phones! But yeah, the gym is unexpectedly closed today."

"Oh, well in that case, good, because I can't be there anyway!" We both laughed.

"Are you busy today?" Megan asked. I was surprised by her question, as we'd never been chatty with each other before.

"No, I just need a break," I said sheepishly.

"Yeah, I get that. I didn't mean to put you on the spot. It's just that my cousin who owns *High Noon Horses* is having an open house today, and they are doing horseback rides to benefit the Whispering Pines Church. I know I've seen you there, so I thought I'd pass it along.

Horseback riding? To benefit my church? Hmm. That must have been what Cody was talking about. Whether or not I wanted to go was another question. While I had been horseback riding once or twice when I was little, it actually sounded kind of fun for a beautiful autumn day. Megan gave me the details, and we hung up.

I decided to call Blair and see if she was going after all. She answered after the third ring.

"Good morning, Ginger." Her voice was raspy, like she'd been sleeping.

"I hope I didn't wake you," the guilt of which felt tremendous.

"No, my eyes had opened a few minutes before you called." There was a laugh in her voice.

"Well, either way, I'm sorry to disturb you. Are you going for a horseback ride today?"

"Oh, is that *today?*" No RSVP ever started with that sentence. "I'm sorry, Ginger. I can't make it. But I think *you* should go. Take pictures. Have a fun experience!" The pep in her voice was contagious and thirty minutes later, I was getting ready to leave.

I was only going because the proceeds were going to be donated to my church, and I had no other plans that day. With church the following day, there would be a small going away party for Cody after the service. From there, we would launch into Pumpkin Stampede prep, and it was going to be a full week.

I excitedly dressed, taking the time to curl my reddish hair into a cowgirl style. Since I'd been on a horse twice in my youth, I felt confident that if I showed up in full western regalia, it would look natural. And that was just what I did.

Checking my reflection in the mirror before I left, my plum-colored cowboy hat matched the flowers on my western button up long sleeve blouse. It was tucked into my Ariat jeans, and my turquoise belt was the cutest addition to the outfit. I gently brushed out the ringlets in my hair, creating dreamy waves of texture. All that was left was my shoe selection.

I had a lot of boots, since my shoe size has been the same since I was in the eighth grade. But what those boots didn't have was any real-western setting experience. I honestly had no idea which one was right for riding; so I settled on a square toe cowboy boot—my newer ones I had picked up a year earlier at the western store. They were *FatBaby by Ariat* and had beautiful turquoise stitching and completed the outfit well. I opted for no jewelry other than post earrings—it wasn't a fashion show, after all. It was a riding lesson. "Yeehaw!" I snapped a picture of my look and posted it to my social media. If I was going to be a cowgirl, I needed to post like one, too. The imposter syndrome quickly took over, and I opted against posting the photo online.

Small Town Wisdom

Whenever you dress up in theme, add one more item. That way, you have something to discard of later when you realize the outfit isn't as good as you thought it was.

When I arrived at the arena, no one was at the front desk inside. There was no bell to ring, so I peeked my head down the hallway and saw light spilling out from an open office door. I thought I heard someone speaking, so I walked towards the door, reaching my hand up to knock on it when I saw it was empty. The sound was coming from elsewhere.

High Noon Horses were on beautiful grounds that backed up to a forest. There were trail markers all around it, with ratings of difficulty for each. It was a horse training facility that also boarded horses and occasionally sold them.

Entering the arena main floor, I saw someone walking through with a hay bale. "Hey, there. I'm here for the horseback rides benefiting Whispering Pines Church. Where is everybody?" The man motioned over his shoulder with his head.

"They are outside right now working on a sale. But I think Jenny, who's assigning the horses, is out there, too, so feel free to head on outside."

I thanked him and headed out the back door that was propped open with a stack of horseshoes. Sure enough, there was a gal wearing a nametag that read *Jenny*, a few wranglers and... Tucker?

"This horse here would be the perfect one for a brute such as yourself. It's steady, but a little bit of a wild child. He doesn't fear a thing in the world, which is both good and bad if you know what I mean." Tucker appeared to be in the middle of a sales pitch when I walked up, unsure if I should take his hand, his arm, or just stand beside him, so I did the latter.

"Hey," I interjected, seeing the pretend man in my life talking to a wrangler. The man quickly took one look at me up and down and held his hand out.

"Boone Miller, at your service." He shook my hand longer than socially acceptable, and I pulled it away with a laugh.

"Ginger. Nice to meet you." I got a strange vibe from Boone, and I stood a little closer to Tucker because of it. Boone's eyes went wild.

"You two...?" He pointed a finger and me and Tucker.

"Yes, that's right," I piped up fast, and Tucker didn't react. I was hoping he would pick up on the situation when he put his arm around me. Relief washed over me.

"Okay, then. Ginger, tell your *boyfriend* that he needs Ace here." Boone rubbed his hand on the side of the black stallion's chest. "He's a real beaut. We got him from an auction for another rider who ended up getting a mule. Go figure." Boone rolled his eyes.

Tucker was horse shopping? I guess I knew so little about Tucker that it was starting to be embarrassing. But then again, where would he keep it while he was living in a motel?

"I didn't know you were in the market for a horse... Honey," I said in the most endearing tone I could possibly muster. Tucker grinned.

"I'm not. But Boone here," Tucker said in a tone I didn't recognize, "thinks I need one anyway. And even offered to let me board him here free of charge." It was then that I realized Tucker was speaking with a barbed civility. Were these two men feeling *competitive* against one another?

"Alright, alright. Well, I've got a date with your girl Ginger here. You mull it over and get back to me."

I was partially pleased that Boone had called the sales pitch off but was also horrified that I might be the only one riding with him. Boone handed the reins to Jenny, who seemed perfectly content to talk to Tucker some more.

"Want to ride him around here and see what you think?" Jenny asked Tucker in a flirtatious tone, but I didn't get to hear his answer because Boone motioned for us to go to the horses.

"I've got our horses waiting for us over here. Since it's still early, it's just going to be you and Mary over there." Boone pointed at a woman whom I'd seen in passing at church but wasn't formally acquainted with. I was relieved I wasn't the only one going out with Boone, and something in my gut was fighting the idea of it.

"Okay, sure. Nice to meet you, Mary." My voice had no hope in it whatsoever, but no one ever seemed to pick up on those emotional cues, so I let it go. When I saw the horses, neither of them were the small, pony-like types I remembered from my childhood. Instead, one of them was clawing at the ground like he was about to charge me, and the other one was impossibly huge, like a draft horse.

"Uh, no ponies today?" I asked, as Boone led the angsty horse over to the gate.

"Nope. Those are just for beginners." My eyes widened.

"But I *am* a beginner...?" I looked at him in disbelief.

"And we're about to change that, aren't we, *Reaper?*" He pulled out a carrot from his vest pocket and gave it to the jet-black horse.

"So, let me get this straight," my voice was trembling as I spoke, "you have me riding a horse named '*Reaper*'?" I reminded myself I didn't have to do anything I didn't want to do. But while considering that it was for a good cause, I wrestled with that train of thought.

"Yep. He's a great pack horse. Just don't do anything to tick him off."

"And what would that consist of?" I croaked.

"Don't insult his intelligence or tell him he ain't as pretty as my boy Scorch over here, for one." Boone motioned to his larger-than-life draft horse. He was a reddish dark brown with a black mane, and it looked like he was wearing black socks. He was a beautiful animal, with a towering presence. "You can get on Reaper by using the gate to his pen. Here, watch me." Boone led Scorch to the rim of the pen, took one step onto the bars of the gate, while his other foot went into a stirrup, and he swung his tall leg over in one fluid motion. He was so high up, I had to bend my neck all the way just to see him up there.

As Boone turned Scorch around to get out of my way, I felt a gaze on me. Looking back over my shoulder, Tucker was now in the saddle on Ace, and I felt a twinge in my chest. Tucker was a cowboy, that much was obvious. But seeing him on a horse made me feel things I wasn't ready for. I felt my cheeks redden as his gaze intensified, watching my every move. Turning, I got another look at Reaper, as Mary was getting on a saddled white horse. I was the hold out. I reached my hand out to Reaper, and he snorted, showing his teeth around the bit in his mouth.

It was now or never. "C'est la vie," I said, mumbling a prayer under my breath. "Lord, I have no idea what I am doing here. I am putting my trust in an animal, and I pray you keep me safe." I did just as Boone had shown me, stepping on the gate with one leg, bringing me up to height, then getting a leg into the stirrup. It worked beautifully. My heart was pounding a million beats per minute, and it seemed too scary to take my attention off of the horse's movements for even a second to turn around and see if Tucker was still watching me, but I felt his eyes still. And I was surprised at how comforting that was.

"Okay, giddy up. Reaper will follow me, and Mary? Your Daisy will follow, too," Boone spoke firmly, his horse stomping a little as he tried to get him going. "I don't know what has gotten into you, Scorch." Thankfully, Reaper kept somewhat of a distance behind Boone, as it did appear something had gotten into Scorch. He was acting agitated, as Reaper had moments before, but my horse had settled down. As we started along the tree-lined trail, I was pleased with how flat it was and prayed it would continue. But not even sixty seconds into our ride, Scorch went up on his back legs, rearing and letting out a loud squeal, and its hooves pawed at the sky. Boone held on, impressively, but I felt fear take over that he or the horse may fall. It was just such a large animal.

For a split second, I forgot I was sitting on a horse of my own. The reins that had been gently sitting in my palm were accidentally pulled on as I moved my hands to my body in surprise. Reaper, reacting to me tugging his reins and Boone hollering to Scorch, took off in a fast trot, spooked by the ordeal. I tried to remain calm; I was pretty sure horses could smell fear. For those short few seconds, it felt very dramatic, like I was in a runaway train car on a cliffside. I started rambling off all of the things associated with horses to see if there was a magic word that would make him stop, as tugging on the reins did nothing. "Woah, woah," nope. "Easy now!" Nothing. "Please, Reaper- Stop!" Reaper slowed, stopping at the base of a pine tree. Whew. My body was shaking from the adrenaline. I wasn't that far off from where Boone was, but I wasn't sure if he was still on Scorch. I tried to turn my body, but I felt really stiff from the shock.

Reaper, standing next to the pine tree, took a step forward. "Hey, now. What are we doing?" His head was under the lowest branch. I pulled back on the reins instinctively, but he didn't move an inch. "Okay, let's go back, Reaper." I tried the reins again. Nothing. Just then, he took another step forward. The branch was now up to the saddle horn. I took my feet out of the stirrups as if I was going to do an Olympian acrobatic dismount from this horse, when I struggled using a step ladder to reach a box of cereal in my cabinet above the fridge. "Reaper, don't go any farther, buddy." Maybe being his friend would work? My body broke out into a sweat. I didn't know what to do there, but I didn't have too many options left. I finally turned when I heard hooves coming up behind me at a fast pace, but before I could see who it was, Reaper bolted forward, sling-shotting me off the horse.

When I opened my eyes, I was laying on my back in the dirt. "Ginger? Ginger! Are you okay?" It was Tucker. He dismounted from Ace and kneeled at my side, Reaper nowhere to be seen. I managed to sit up, assessing my body for injuries.

"Oh no..." I croaked.

"What is it? Is something broken? Do you need an ambulance?" Tucker gently held my upper body with his arm behind me.

"No, I think I'm okay. But I think I ruined my boots." The leather was scratched from one end to the other. "And where is my hat?" I felt the void on top of my head. Tucker let out a laugh.

"As long as you didn't ruin that brain of yours," he joked, as he slowly helped me to my feet. "Your hat is right here." He set it back on my hair, which was filled with pine needles. I was trembling from the experience, filled with adrenaline. "Do you want to ride Ace back, or walk?"

"If I never get on a horse again, it will be too soon." I gave him a look as I nearly fell again to my knees, feeling weak. I hadn't eaten breakfast that morning, and with the added excitement, it was all too much.

"Okay, let's get you back. Here, I got you." Tucker, with one arm behind my neck, and the other going behind my knees, swooped me off my feet like I weighed nothing. He didn't even appear to struggle as he made the walk back to the corral, which had to have been at least 100 yards. If I hadn't felt so lethargic…

Back at the corral, Tucker set me down on the tailgate of his pickup truck. "I'm sorry to be like this. I think I just need to eat." I lifted my arm up to feel my forehead, and I felt sweaty. Dehydrated. Starving.

"They don't call me the muffin man for nothin', Ginger." Tucker walked to the front of his truck and pulled out a bag of treats, handing me an apple fritter donut.

"Yikes. Did Laney tell you her nickname for you? And if you're planning on adopting that as your official title, can I put you down for my emergency contact?" I asked sheepishly as I tore into the donut, its sugary sweetness and fluffy core melting in my mouth.

"Blair mentioned it to me in passing. You girls are hilarious," Tucker said, hands on his waist as I ate the delicate donut. "And go ahead and write me in for that. At this point, you're taking a fall every few days. It will give me something to do in my off hours."

Favorite Fall Recipes (when skipping the gym)
Anything in a five-mile vicinity will do.
A pinch of salt.

"What can I say? You being in town brings out the worst behavior in me." Taking another bite, my eyes closed as I experienced the fresh, sweet apple chunks and buttery pecan bits. Once again, my body felt rejuvenated by baked goods, and I was back on my feet a few moments later, but not without a wave of dizziness.

Jenny appeared with a bottle of water. "How is she doing?" Jenny whispered to Tucker as I drank it.

"She got tossed off that horse of yours, and she had low blood sugar. But otherwise, I think she'll be alright." His tone was firm, and Jenny nodded.

"I'm so sorry that happened, Ginger. I better go start looking for Reaper." Jenny pulled a mule out of the corral, threw a saddle on it, and made her way towards the trail.

"Ace is still out there, too," Tucker called after her, while Megan just gave a thumbs up without looking back.

"Where is Boone?" I asked. Tucker shrugged.

"I think he's inside nursing his wounds."

"Did he get hurt?" I asked. I missed the aftermath of his horse rearing up.

"Just his ego. It reared up a few times and he got off of it in time, thankfully. But who takes a draft horse on a trail ride?" Tucker asked rhetorically. I didn't know the difference, just that the horse was the biggest one I'd ever seen. We were both quiet for a minute. "Look, I'm sorry. I shouldn't have insulted him like that. I am disappointed he would put you in danger, though, by giving you the horse he did and being too distracted to notice." Tucker's words felt *validating.* I knew the moment I saw Reaper that it was the wrong horse for me to be taking out with my less than three hours experience with horses. Mary was to my right, brushing Daisy in the corral.

"Thank you for being there. If you hadn't been, I'd still be out there probably." I took another sip of my water, sitting back on the tailgate of his truck. "Why were you here, anyway?"

"I came to drop off some pies for Jenny. She's having a party tonight." I raised my eyebrows in an unspoken bout of interest, wondering if she invited Tucker to said party. "Anyway,

I saw the whole thing happen, and I gotta say, you did everything right that you could. When I came up, you were pulling back on the reins. It's not your fault he went forward, but when he did, your feet were out of the stirrups and the reins out of your hands. Because there was nothing to tangle you up, you gracefully slid off."

"It sure didn't feel graceful. I feel like I popped a muscle in my butt." I readjusted how I was sitting because it was uncomfortable on my sore glutes.

"Yeah, I bet you'll have some aches and pains for a while. I'm just saying, you're a cowgirl if I ever saw one..." Tucker took a step toward me. His rugged muscles looked like they were going to pop out of his shirt after carrying me all that way, and I liked it. The feeling between us was electrified at that moment. I didn't know what came over me, but suddenly, I wanted to be kissed by him. There was only a foot between us, so I started to lean in. And when Tucker did the same, I closed my eyes, ready to feel the spark of my lips on his.

"Now, now. Don't get too comfortable. We still have a horseback ride to take, Ginger." Boone walked up at an uncomfortably close distance, taking charge of the situation and, it seemed, he was trying to get my attention back on him. If that was the case, I was partially flattered, but my interest in Tucker at that moment peaked.

"If it's alright, I think I'll cancel my ride today. I've had enough excitement for one morning," Boone's expression was unreadable. I couldn't tell if he was accepting of my cancelling or not.

"We have a non-refundable policy. You'll have to buy another ride if you want to go again." It was clear. Boone had a bit of a 'tude going, and I didn't appreciate it.

"Well, in that case..." My voice trailed off. "Thank you for your time. It's been an interesting experience, to say the least." I didn't mean my words to come off as such a diss and regretted the tone. But I also didn't appreciate how he was speaking to me, and I had a feeling it had everything to do with Tucker being there. I said goodbye to Tucker and got up from the tailgate. As I started to walk towards the front of the arena where my car was, Boone called out.

"Ginger? I suppose just this once I can reschedule our ride, since we did have a hiccup, and all." I turned to look at him. He looked... desperate.

"Thanks, but no thanks, Boone." When I got to my car, I half expected Tucker to come knock on my window and finish what we started, though my feelings were cooling off. As I drove back home, I was actually relieved that we hadn't kissed. That would have made things messier than necessary, and I just didn't need that complication then. It was good to remember that none of it with Tucker was real, and he and I were using each other as a stand-in to get what we really wanted. Though Dallas's appeal was quickly waning, I would never admit it to Tucker.

*****

The next morning, feeling freshly shampooed and free of pine needles, I got ready for church. It was going to be a long day filled with Pumpkin Stampede prep as I was on the booth committee, and we had our going away party for Cody. My heart went out to Blair; I started brainstorming ideas of things to keep her mind off of his absence while he was gone for the next twelve months, and knew we needed to plan a little engagement celebration, bridal shower and wedding. The thought thrilled me; I wanted nothing more than for Blair to marry her sweetheart, and I couldn't wait to celebrate with her.

I chose a knee length, burnt orange dress and wore a cream-colored long sleeve shirt underneath. It looked really cute and was extremely cozy. I wore thick, wooly socks and a pair of cream-colored Old Gringo cowboy boots that I picked up at a second hand store a year earlier. Those boots were a dream, and every time I wore them, I wondered why they weren't my daily boots. They were so flattering on the foot, and the stitching was meticulous.

My hair was soft and slippery that morning, so I put it half up with a sunflower hair clip. I looked like a walking advertisement for autumn, and I didn't hate it.

When I arrived at the white steepled building, most of our small congregation had already arrived. I usually sat toward the front, but all of the pews were full, so I ended up in the very back row, smack dab in the center. We had a short intro of music, which I loved, as Cody's sister Melody was playing the harp, and then Cody got started with his very timely sermon of following God's call, not our own. I was moved to tears as Cody explained he would love nothing more than to stay there with his family and our congregation, but God wasn't done writing his story. When his sermon was over, and Melody started back on the harp to a song I didn't recognize, it was then that I noticed how nice he was dressed. Maybe it had to do with him not being able to wear a suit for the next twelve months as he schlepped through the jungle spreading the gospel, but he looked great in his black suit and green tie that matched his eyes. His brown, wavy hair was perfectly gelled. His shoes shined. I scanned the pews for Blair, but I didn't see her. My eyes instead stumbled upon Tucker, who had his elbows on his knees as he prayed.

"Many of you know that we are having a small reception here for my going away party." Cody's began talking while Melody continued playing her harp. "But what you don't know, and what I'd love for you to be a part of if you're able, is that Blair and I wish to be married. Today. Right now, actually. So, if you'll stand for the bride..." My jaw dropped. Tears fell from my eyes as the chapel doors swung open right behind me and Blair, standing next to her father, walked in.

She was the most beautiful bride I'd ever laid eyes on. Her white dress had long sleeves, a short train and delicate buttons all the way up her back. Her shiny, black hair was adorned with the smallest white flowers, and, in pure Blair fashion, she was wearing white high heel shoes. I couldn't believe it; they were eloping in the most amazing, infamous way possible and not leaving a single person out of their joy. I was over the moon.

Blair's father turned out to be the minister, having just gotten ordained the day before online. And afterwards, I couldn't wait to wish them well. With Cody leaving in just two days, I couldn't think of anything more romantic for them.

Tucker wheeled out a white cake, and I nearly toppled over when I heard he was hired to make it and sworn to secrecy. "You should've told me!" I said to Tucker, before I waited to congratulate my dearest friends as they made their rounds.

"Hello to you too, darlin'," Tucker smirked, crossing his arms. "I made a promise, and I intend to keep all of those." He shrugged and smiled. I couldn't blame him for that.

"That was very good of you. I guess I just wish I had been in on it, too. I wouldn't have worn this cream color today, for one." I laughed it off as I looked around the room. "Is it still a faux pas to wear white if we didn't know we were attending a wedding?" Tucker mumbled something under his breath that I couldn't make out. "What was that?"

"Sorry, I'm exhausted. I was up at the Pumpkin Perk Cafe until the wee hours trying to finish frosting this cake, plus three sheet cakes for the congregation. I'm wiped."

"Need any taste testers for it?" I asked, as people were standing around waiting for it to be served.

"Not this one. This is a vanilla cake with buttercream frosting. It's still great, don't get me wrong. But how can you mess up vanilla?" he laughed.

"You clearly haven't had any of my baking..." I shivered remembering a pie I tried to make once out of apples I had picked. The crust was really soggy, and the apples turned to mush. "Besides, I have something special just for you in the cooler. When we're done here, before the committee meets, maybe you can help me push these carts back to the kitchen and then you can try it?"

"I'd love that! How you find time to do it all amazes me." Between Blair's surprise nuptials, Megan's bridal shower, all of the town's harvest parties, and his own business, how he had time to still make something new for me to sample really was impressive. Plus, he was a beautiful looking man with a really strong upper body. I started wondering what his workout routine entailed for him to be able to carry me like I was nothing, when I remembered I was standing in the house of the Lord, and I needed to focus on the things happening around me.

Blair and Cody finally reached Tucker and me in the room. Immediately, Blair and I embraced in a deep hug. "I am so, so happy for you. You are the most beautiful bride." I didn't want to let go of her, but then it was my turn to hug Cody. When our embrace ended, I looked at them both. "There could never be a better pairing than this."

"I'm sorry I didn't tell you, Ginger. Laney didn't even know until late last night because my dad left the screen up on his computer." We all chuckled.

"I totally understand, Blair. This was all so perfect, and how very romantic." Blair and Cody embraced.

"He really is romantic." Blair let a tear fall from her eye. "I just love him so much, and I'm so blessed to be his wife." Cody wiped the tears from his eyes, and I prayed right then and there for my own love story.

Lord, I want this, too. Nothing short of it. Because the love that You ordain is beautiful.

Amen.

I could tell Tucker felt moved by their love, too, when he reached for my hand and squeezed it. The lines were starting to blur, and the nagging voice in the back of my head reminded me of Tucker's prompt: "*No falling in love.*"

*****

After the bride and groom left, family of Blair and Cody stayed behind to help clean up the small event hall in the back of the chapel. I helped Tucker clean up the cake trays. We didn't have hardly any cake leftover, except for a piece for Blair and Cody to put in their freezer for their first wedding anniversary when he returned. Laney ended up leaving with that to make sure it didn't get eaten, because Tucker's cakes were a huge hit! He may have been modest while describing the cakes, but no one did vanilla like that man.

When we got all the frosting off the carts, the trays cleared from their crumbs and the sinks wiped up from their sugary debris, Tucker walked to the kitchen cooler and pulled out a small pink box, wrapped in twine, with a plastic fork wrapped up in the bow.

"You really do think of everything, don't you?" I laughed, pulling the string and opening the box. Inside was a beautiful piece of what looked like classic pumpkin pie.

"This right here," he pointed to the pie slice, "is the one. For the bake-off. I really think so, anyway. So, take a bite and tell me what you think, darlin'." I noticed my cheeks got hot every time he referred to me as "darlin'" as an involuntary reflex.

"Oh, really? Okay, let's dig in, then!" I got a healthy piece of the pie and its crust on my fork. After several samplings of all of his fun creations, such as pumpkin cheesecake, pumpkin praline, cinnamon apple pumpkin, and so on, I was pretty surprised that he was going with a classic pumpkin pie for the bake-off. That was until the flavors hit my lips.

Silky pumpkin, nutty crust, and that secret-spice ingredient from before, but bolder. The flavors were an exaggeration in the best way-—that pie tasted like a candied version of the classic, but with buttery nostalgia and a modern twist. "Tucker, you've really done it. You are right—this is the pie." I took another bite, wanting to pace myself as my piece was smaller than usual, and I wanted to savor it. "It reminds me of...

gingerbread?" I couldn't get enough. So much for savoring, since the slice was gone quicker than I intended, as I picked up the flaky crust with my fingers.

Ginger's Polished Thoughts

Keep your nailbeds nice. You never know when you'll be eating desserts with your hands.

"That's my secret ingredient," Tucker smiled, arms crossed.

"Will you just tell me what that secret ingredient is? I promise I won't learn to bake and open up a dueling business right next to yours with it," I smiled, licking my fork in the most ladylike way possible.

"You've already guessed it." Tucker looked at me expectantly.

"Oh. Gingerbread?" I asked.

"Ginger," He winked. "I have found that using ginger creates the most unexpected twist to my classic recipes."

*****

After Blair and Cody were sent off, and everyone wished them well, the realization sunk in that we wouldn't see Cody for a year. Our assistant pastor, Henry, would be filling in for him while he was gone. Henry was overseeing today's committee, and though we were all full of the sugary, sweet wedding cake, and I had even more dessert, the vibe was tiring. I felt exhausted. Overwhelmed. Instead of the normal excitement for the Pumpkin Stampede—our biggest event of the year as a community—that year, it felt like a lot was riding on it.

As our church committee worked for the rest of the afternoon on getting our booths set up, Tucker and I kept sharing stolen glances. At one point, my head was down as I was touching up paint on a sign, and I looked up and saw him smiling at me. New feelings were replacing my doubts; and I was throwing out the caution with the leaves blowing by in the wind.

CHAPTER 8:
THE SCENT OF CINNAMON, A HINT OF HIM

October 1st may as well have been a bank holiday in Maple Haven, because you'd be hard pressed to find a single business open, at least during the parade. On the tree-lined main street that was swarming in flaming aspens, Canadian reds, and brightly colored maples at every turn, it was decked out in the natural decor that the colorful trees brought, but absolutely dazzled by the rest. Everywhere you looked had piles of bright orange pumpkins, festive sundried haybales, string lighted garlands, buckets of apples, and fresh pressed cider barrels inside every business. The one thing our town could agree on was the beauty of autumn, paired with the fresh chill in the air, and finally, the Pumpkin Stampede was there.

Blair, fresh from taking Cody to the airport, was bleary-eyed and happy crying all morning. Laney and I were comforting her as we had three chairs sitting a block down from the salon in front of The Pumpkin Perk Cafe, where we were at the end in a cul-de-sac. We were at the very front of the parade, as all of the floats lined up one street over and when they came around the corner, there we were. Everyone in the procession was wearing their autumn best: oranges, corals, yellows, teals and browns, if not a full-blown pumpkin costume. The mayor, Billy Blanks, was the Grand Marshall, who not only led the parade, but would also follow any group with horses, pushing a wheelbarrow to make sure the streets were left in pristine condition. Not only that, but he was dressed like a scarecrow and always made people laugh.

" *The Cozy Cuticle* may be the only business in town that isn't represented here, ladies," Laney quipped, while I shook my head profusely, feeling the wind nipping at my cheeks.

"That's where I draw the line. I do not want to be in the parade. Someone has to spectate." I took a sip of my pumpkin chai coffee that Tucker had made me that morning before he shut down his truck. It was then that I realized I didn't know where he went.

"Where's Tucker?" Laney asked, as Bruce came by with a folding chair and set up shop next to her.

"That's a great question. Maybe he's watching from across the street?" I peered through the crowds as the Pumpkin Queen made her procession through in the backseat of a pink

Cadillac driven by Lexie Blair. She was sitting up on top of the back and waving, her hair in a perfect blowout with her orange tiara *almost* brighter than her spray tan. It was an unspoken rule that to be a Pumpkin Queen, you must have a fake-baked tan, as every single woman who previously had the crown had sought after one immediately. That year's reigning Pumpkin Queen was in her final event, and I waved at Lexie, who was driving her.

The topic of Tucker was quickly forgotten when a *Ram 3500* pulling a flatbed trailer slowly rode by. On the back of the trailer was Dallas, using a lat machine and Megan, holding a sign that read, "*Maple Muscle Gym.*"

"Well, well, well. Okay, I get it, Ginger," Laney laughed, and I nearly toppled over in my lawn chair with the shock from her acknowledging Dallas. I knew Laney and Blair didn't think Dallas was *ugly,* but while we all giggled and Bruce pretended to gag, Dallas noticed me in the crowd, stopped what he was doing, and *waved.* I would have liked to have said it took more than a wave to impress me. I really, really would have. But I just couldn't, because it excited me to no end that he did.

A few minutes later, while I was lost in my thoughts about Dallas, another float came by for an outfitting company. The trailer it was built upon creaked as it slid by us. They were followed by a band of riders on horseback who were walking in a synchronized pattern. I looked at each person who went by, when I gasped: Tucker was in the group, riding a white paint horse with brown spots. Everything around me went silent. It felt like only Tucker and me existed in the world. He expertly moved his horse around in the formation, trotting side to side, and in mere moments, would stand right next to me. His horse towered over me, and I stood to say hello to him as he went by.

"Hi," I hollered out, over the cheers and laughter of the crowd and the volume of the announcer who was getting louder by the second. Tucker smiled and his cheek dimple was everything. My attraction was growing for him like a wildfire in a windstorm.

"Hey, darlin'," he winked, and I thought I might spontaneously combust. Sitting back down, I felt like I was breathless.

"Now we're talking. Am I right, Ginger?" Laney elbowed me to make sure I took it all in as Tucker rode off with the group. His cream, paisley button-up shirt looked crisp and clean, making his tan look even deeper. He was a cowboy through and through. "Now that's a man!" Bruce lifted his hands up in protest.

"Hello, Laney? Your husband is sitting right here, and he has all of his hearing and feelings?" Bruce smirked. Laney and

Bruce had a beautiful relationship, and she loved that man fiercely. They also loved to tease each other.

"Babe, you are the best man in the world, and you're already married to me. So, I gotta help Ginger find hers." That settled things with Bruce, and he was pleased, even adding in some encouragement for me and Tucker.

The excitement of the parade was winding down, since it was the kids' turn to run out and collect all the candy in the street that the last float threw for them. The children ran wild, grabbing up handfuls of bubble gum and lollipops, while we collected our chairs and wandered back to the salon. We stored our chairs in the back room, made sure everything was ready for the day, and opened our doors for business. While we didn't have much on the books, we enjoyed spending some down time together.

Blair, with no appointments scheduled for the next few days, decided that she was going to go home and work on packing, as she was moving into Cody's house, and Laney and I looked at the appointment book.

"So..." Laney trailed off. I knew the moment we were alone she was going to dig in. In fact, I was glad she finally ripped the tape off. "Tonight's the pie bake-off, and tomorrow the rodeo *and* bachelor auction. *And* the hoe-down. What do you say we call our appointments, have them come in now, and close up for the next two days?" I squealed at her good idea.

"I'm already calling my girls now!" I said, furiously dialing Sadie and Millie, my only two appointments for the day. Both needed a fill to their acrylics, and I thought about how fast I could get them done. On my first call, Sadie agreed.

"I have to get these puppies filled- I'm barrel racing tomorrow, and if they were any longer, I probably won't be able to hold onto the reins." Just the thought of holding reins sent a shiver down my spine.

My next phone call, Millie, cancelled.

"I know it's awful timing, but it appears I've come down with the flu bug. I'm set to be missing every single event of the Pumpkin Stampede." Her tears went on for several minutes, but by the sound of her cough, it was the right decision.

When I checked back in with Laney, she was also down to just one appointment. She gave me a high five before we both sank into a pedicure chair, put our feet up and waited for our clients.

"What are you going to do, Ginger?" Laney asked quietly.

I was confused by her question and pushed my eyebrows together. "What do you mean, Laney?"

"About Tucker. I know what's going on here. I know about his past. And I think it's really sweet that you wanted to help him out so he could win this bake-off." I felt the weightlifting from my shoulders instantly. To not be harboring my secret any longer was a dream come true! The last few days had felt torturous trying to keep it inside.

"I don't know. I've just had such a long-standing crush on Dallas. It's hard to turn it off, you know?" Laney nodded.

"I get it. Remember in high school when I thought I liked Dennis?" She let out a chuckle.

"Yes, of course. His curly, orange hair was so cute. Wait—what do you mean you *thought* you liked him? On my end, it seemed like you were head over heels for that guy." Every sleep over we had, Laney was writing him love notes that she never intended to send him.

"I didn't know Dennis at all. Didn't know what he liked, disliked, his thoughts or feelings. The only thing I knew was that he was cute. But looks don't mean a thing, do they?" she asked rhetorically. While she wasn't talking about Dallas, it hit close to home. I knew so little about him, but what I did know, we didn't exactly jive on. For instance, he was doing the Maple Mile Fun Run right then at the lake running track, after working out on a machine during the entirety of the parade which lasted an hour. The man was solid muscle, but was there anything else inside?

"I just want things to happen naturally. Like they did between you and Bruce. I'm so tired of trying so hard." I let it all out. My feelings, the things that weighed me, and it felt amazing. Laney was a great listener, as always.

"They will, Ginger. You just have to let them." With that, Sadie walked in. Laney's client was quick to follow and before we knew it, we were done for the day.

"Good luck at your barrel race, Sadie. I'll be watching from the stands." Sadie thanked me and left. I locked the door behind her, lit up our fall window display, and turned the open sign to "Closed."

"Let's blow this pop stand," Laney cheered, as she grabbed her purse from under her table. As we walked out the back door, I pulled out my set of keys to lock it behind me. "Ginger—", Laney interjected, and I turned, "follow your heart." Seeing my best friend, Laney, stand before me, all grown up and happily married, giving me advice, was everything I didn't know I needed.

*****

With just two hours before the pie bake-off judging began, I texted Tucker three times, but no response. So, I picked up the phone and called him like it was 1995: ringing over and over until he picked up. It worked.

"Hey, Ginger, I'm sorry, I—" I interrupted.

"We've got no time to waste, Tucker. Where are we meeting? This showdown is in less than 120 minutes." I could hear him laughing on the other side of the call.

"Oh, you want to join me for this? I'm calling your side of the bargain complete because one of the judges just asked me if my *girlfriend* is the pretty redhead from the nail salon. Mission accomplished." Hearing Tucker refer to me as his anything made my heart flutter. But yet, he was saying it was over, before "it" had ever even begun?

Favorite Fall Recipes (when your love life feels uncertain)

1 pan of cinnamon rolls from the nearest diner

Give one to your closest gal pal

Eat the remaining 3

Be puffy for 2-6 business days, disappearing from his life

He will wonder where you are and reach out

May work up to 23% of the time

"The bake-off judging hadn't even begun. Shouldn't I have been there in support? I feel like it would be weird if I wasn't." My voice felt shaky. My stomach, uneasy. My heart, unsure.

"Yeah, sure—I suppose you're right about that. If it isn't too much of a hassle, that is. Want to just come down to the county complex? I'm hustling over here at the complex trying to perfect my pie. We each have our own judge watching us make the pies so they can be sure that no one uses 'illegal ingredients.' Whatever that means? I tried to ask them, but all I got was the run around and a story about someone making an alcoholic version."

"Oh, I remember that year! I'll have to tell you that story another time, but the judge was pretty intoxicated after a slice. I'm sorry for interrupting," I laughed. I should have known better than to just let it ring and ring. The man was trying to get his pie just right for the contest. But I couldn't help myself. I was excited.

"You didn't—that's okay. I think it's cute you were so interested in what I'm doing." The tone in his voice was flirtatious, causing my uneasy feeling to surpass.

"I'll let you get to it. See you soon." I hung up the phone, sitting in my feelings.

At the county complex, Tucker's pie was going up against eleven other contestants, to which he was the only man participating. It was actually cute, because the ten competitors were already in their seats at the front table with their pies before Tucker got in. The vibe was hostile; all of those women were ready to hotly contest if their concoction wasn't named the victor. But then, Tucker strolled in, donning his best cowboy regalia that I'd yet seen, and all of the women softened after one look in his direction.

Tucker was dressed to the nines. He was wearing a dark brown hat, a dark tan button up, and dark rinse jeans. His cowboy boots looked like Ostrich leather from where I was sitting. The smooth shine of his golden belt buckle that was covered in fancy script and jewels told me it was a rodeo win. He didn't appear to be nervous, but for some reason, my palms were sweating profusely as I sat in the front row.

The announcer and main judge was a woman named Karen Binks. "Welcome to the 22nd Annual Maple Haven Pumpkin Pie Bake-Off!" The crowd cheered as I looked around, clapping with them. There were well over 300 people in attendance. "We have eleven contestants this year from all over the county. That includes four previous title holders of the best Pumpkin Pie in Maple Haven, with our own Marjorie here winning for five years in a row! Give her a round of applause." Karen excitedly clapped while holding the microphone. "As many of you know, when a winner decides they no longer wish to compete, they get to become a judge of the contest. That means everyone on our judges panel has earned their right to decide what a Maple Haven winning pie tastes like!" The crowd clapped again, but things were starting to settle down, and Karen took the cue.

"Now, let's get started. First up, we have Belinda Marks, hailing from Sage Mountain, Wyoming originally, and a resident of Maple Haven for the last sixteen years. This is her third time competing, and this year, she made an apple spiced pumpkin pie. It has two layers of crust and a cinnamon center. A little bit less traditional, but Belinda enjoys creating one-of-a-kind creations and never follows a recipe!" Karen was reading off of a card and when she got to the last sentence, her eyes grew wide. "Oh dear, no recipe? Well! Good luck, Belinda!" The judges were each given a small sliver of her pie, and while the description sounded amazing, the faces they made told another story altogether. I couldn't help but giggle when the last judge took a bite and pretended she was wiping her mouth but obviously spit it out instead. I knew the feeling when trying to be discreet backfired.

After each sample was tasted by the judges, they spent a few minutes writing notes. There was one particular judge that

I found interesting—she wasn't taking any notes or making expressions, good or bad. It was very hard to read her face.

Next up, after a long-winded description that I quickly tuned out, was a vanilla cream pumpkin spice pie. The judges seemed overall favorable of t that pie, with some nodding, smiling, or even giving a thumbs up after tasting it. The heat was on. I'd tasted Tucker's pies, and I was confident that he was a gifted baker, but we still had eight more pies to go.

Tucker's creation was the last to go, which was torturous, and he looked at me nervously when they read his information.

"Last, but not least, we have a pie entry from Tucker Callahan! You may know him from the Sweet Pumpkin Pie and All Things Delicious truck in town. This former bull rider turned baker has lots of divine concoctions up his sleeve, but today, he is presenting what he calls a 'classic pumpkin pie,' because he notes, 'that's what this contest is all about.' You got that right, Tucker!" Karen clapped as the pieces of his pie were given to the judges. I was on the edge of my seat watching them. From the most revealing woman in the middle, whom I knew exactly which ones she liked and didn't like, to the nearly-expressionless woman on the end who had yet to give anything away, I was making myself dizzy turning my head so fast.

As they started to bite into it, I remembered tasting it yesterday. Its crust alone could have won that contest. Or the fact that he didn't use a puree—he only used fresh pumpkin in his pies. The silkiness of the pumpkin was mind blowing. The ginger was delicate and danced around with the cinnamon on your senses. Just thinking about the pie made my mouth water. I stole a glance at Tucker, expecting him to be just as wrecked watching as I was, but he was looking at me.

The corners of his lips turning upward, I knew what was just about to follow; a wink from him made all of the skin on my face and neck feel hot. He really was a dreamboat. How on earth could I have ever compared that guy to Dallas?

Oh, Dallas. Gorgeous? Yes. Did he know it? Absolutely. Did I like who he was as a person? It pained me to admit it, but no. We had nothing in common. Completely different interests. And it also took a flat out lie to get him to notice me in any way.

"The judges will now deliberate!" Karen announced, breaking me out of my daydream. What? Wait! I missed all of their reactions because I was so consumed with my own drama! I looked back at Tucker who stood and was shaking the hands of the other contestants. The youngest one of them was still at least thirty years older than Tucker, but you could tell how cute they all thought he was. One was flipping her hair ever so casually, and another, I saw readjust her eyeglasses and straighten her collar before she met him.

Watching Tucker interact with them made me realize what a sweet guy he was. He was not someone I would have to restrict my diet for to get him to notice me. In fact, he didn't like that at all. I wouldn't have to pretend to be someone or something that I was not for him. I wouldn't have to change for a guy like Tucker.

I stood up. What had I been doing all that time? Tucker saw me and gave a confused look, leaving the group of disappointed ladies and walking over.

"Are you okay? You look confused." He read me like a newspaper.

"Oh, umm..." I *was* confused. "I just remembered I forgot to unplug my curling iron at home. I'll be right back." I turned, running out, and Tucker called out after me.

"They announce the winner in twenty minutes..."

"I'll be right back!" I yelled back. I ran out of the complex. What had I done? I ran to my car, realizing my hair was straight that day, which totally blew my cover. I leaned my head on the steering wheel and said a prayer.

Lord, I have been so foolish and self-centered. Putting on this ruse for Dallas, a man that I have to conform myself for?

If I had been able to see past my own selfish desires or recognize my personal body image issues, maybe I could have noticed someone good, like Tucker. Now, I am both excited and afraid of everything this man stands for. He sees me for who I am, my flaws and my strengths, but we agreed that this wouldn't happen—that we wouldn't develop feelings, and here I am Lord. I fear this all was a giant mistake, and had I just gotten to know him for real, this could have been the beginning of our love story. But I am just so hardheaded, Lord. And flawed. And jealous. And a control freak. And I always, always want what I can't have. So, here I am Lord. Broken by my own lies. Confused by my feelings. Completely, madly, freely ready to heal and wanting things to be real with Tucker Callahan.

I lifted my head out of my prayer and looked all around me. I was so thankful for all of my blessings in my life, and yet, I tried to undermine God by trying to force things to happen with Dallas. All at once, it all seemed so silly. And it might have worked out that I'd broken my own heart in the process.

Looking at the clock, the twenty minutes were nearly up. I got out of my car, threw my keys back in my fringe purse, and ran inside. Tucker was standing on stage with a blue ribbon pinned to his shirt and taking a group picture with the judges. *I missed it.* He won, but I wasn't there for him. I knew I had been acting self-centered, but that was the icing on the cake; how could've I ever had anything real if I didn't put the focus on them, even in their big moment? Tucker and I made eye contact, and I smiled, to which he tipped his hat at me. That was it. The end of our arrangement.

Sneaking back out of the event, an emptiness took over me. I needed to right my wrongs. Laney knew what we did, and Blair would know soon, too, as I didn't want to pile it on top of all of her other things right then. But I got a wild hair and decided I would go and see Dallas to tell him the truth, apologize, and let him know I was not interested in him, considering he did ask me out on a date. Right?

When I pulled up to Maple Muscle Gym, there were only two cars in the newly-asphalted parking lot. It appeared even the usual gym-rats (myself included) were out partaking in the festivities that day, but I had a hunch that Dallas was there. I walked in, and Megan wasn't at the front desk. There was no bell to ring, but I saw lights on down the hallway of offices.

"Hello?" I called out, but nobody answered me. I walked down the hallway, looking for anyone who might be there, as the doors were open and lights were on, so I knew the gym was open, when I stumbled upon a scene I wasn't expecting. I turned away, apologizing, and ran back down the hall.

"I'm sorry, I was mistaken to come down here." Dallas came out of the office, while Megan followed.

"Ginger?" he called out after me, but I was already halfway out the front door.

I couldn't get into my car fast enough. My heart raced with adrenaline. Dallas and *Megan? Kissing?* I wasn't sure that the image would ever get out of my head. He came into my salon so I would look at his rank toenail when all along, he was interested in Megan? Ugh. Did I just act completely insane in there?

By the time I pulled into my driveway, I was filled with confusion. I couldn't explain Megan's sparkling diamond ring, and I knew Dallas wasn't engaged. That would have been known to the world. Engagements, weddings, and babies in our community were the talk of the town, and I didn't remember hearing anything about Megan or Dallas. That was something else entirely. Once I was inside and had kicked off my boots, I changed into some of my comfiest pajamas, grabbed a giant bowl, and filled it with sugary cereal and cold milk.

My feelings for Dallas had never been real. I was just as shallow as he was. Realizations were swirling around my mind as things became settled. My phone chimed; I checked it in record time, thinking maybe Tucker wanted to talk to me, but it wasn't him; instead, it was an automated message from my cell phone carrier that my plan has been renewed. *Ugh.* It was four in the afternoon, and the bachelor auction was that night at 6 p.m. sharp. Was I going to pull myself together and see the woman who would win a date with Tucker? I sat up from my slump on the couch, seeing pieces of cereal fall off of my bathrobe out of the corner of my eye. Nah, that would probably just send me down a jealous spiral once again, like when that pretty waitress was unabashedly flirting with him. *Lord, help my feelings. This auction is for charity.* A cool, calm wave of peace came over me. What if Tucker was "won" by a woman who didn't turn out to be his future wife, and it really was just for a good cause?

I admitted, the setup of the evening wasn't great for my mental health, but if I really wanted to rely on the Lord for my peace, I needed to let it go. Come what may. My future husband was out there, somewhere, and if I would quit trying to force things on my own, maybe the Lord would send him my way.

At 5:30 p.m., I realized I had never missed a Pumpkin Stampede week event before. Was it really the year to break tradition? In my own personal bargaining, I decided that I could attend and also *not* be weird about it. So, I changed into a nice outfit, redid my liquid foundation makeup, applied a little face sculpting bronzer, as the sugary cereal did a number on my face puffiness, and brushed my teeth. After that week, I'd be lucky if I didn't have any cavities!

The sunset was spectacular as I drove from my house back to the county complex. Its orange hues were painted with red and pink streaks jetting across the open sky. Fluffy clouds created dramatic shadowy effects throughout, and the last of the fall colors dazzled on the grove of trees. "God, You are so good to me," I said, as the beauty of the sunset brought tears to my eyes.

Small Town Wisdom

Beauty only gets you so far in a small town. A good casserole at the church potluck makes up for a magnitude of faults.

When I arrived at the county complex, the parking lot was full. Hmm. That was okay; there was another lot behind it—except that one was full, too! Never in all of my years in Maple Haven did I remember not being able to find a parking spot for any one of the Pumpkin Stampede events.

I ended up parking in the back of my salon and walking five blocks to the complex. Groups of people all around me were doing the same, and I wondered what was happening that night?

Where were all of those people from? Usually, those events were just attended by our county, except for the rodeo, that was. When I got back to the main building and parking lot, I saw it: a large amount of the license plates were from Sage Mountain, WY, where Tucker was from. Could I have been walking into a bear's den of women from his past? Nah, I didn't get the vibe from Tucker that he had a lot of ex-girlfriends. He was gorgeous, all right, but he seemed too sweet and kind to be that kind of guy.

Walking into the building, I didn't see anyone I recognized at first. Scanning the crowd for *anyone* who was familiar enough to chat with was tough, and attending a bachelor auction alone felt a little... *awkward.* I was elated when someone tapped me on the shoulder, and I turned to see Tucker.

"Hi!" I leaned in and gave him a hug, our first embrace. He hugged me back, hard. My head was at his chest. *I needed that.* Not wanting to let go, but realizing it would be weird if I didn't, I slowly stepped back. "Congrats on your win. I am so sorry I was outside when they announced; I must have lost track of time," I stammered.

"They announced a little early... And thank you. I couldn't have done it without your help." I felt nervous. Shaky. My shallow mind noticed how hot he looked, but I swatted those thoughts away. If I had any chance of something real, it needed to be about the person, not about looks—his or mine.

"So, big night tonight, huh?" I asked.

"Yeah, I don't know why, but this whole thing just doesn't sit well with me." He trailed off while I held my breath in hope—could he not want to because he had feelings for me, too? "All of my buddies drove up here just so they could tease me about it." He let out a laugh as he pointed to a group of cowboys standing at the refreshments table. All of them were tall, handsome, and rugged just like Tucker. My eyes widened. *Had the director of the event seen who else was out there? They could make a fortune for the food pantry if any of those men were single,* I thought as I laughed to myself.

"How nice of them to come and support you." Smiling, he laughed again.

"They are jerks. All of them. I think actually they are hoping that they can be auctioned off with me. I know more than four of them are ready to meet a woman, but back in Sage Mountain, it's like three men to one woman..."

"So, you're saying the odds of meeting a man in Sage Mountain are pretty good?" I raised my eyebrows, hand on my chin as I contemplated this.

"Yeah, but the goods are odd," he pointed back to his friends as one of them was eating a piece of pumpkin pie with his bare hands like a pizza slice.

"Maybe Sage Mountain and Maple Haven need to plan a singles mixer. I think we have it the other way around—way more women here than there are men!" I looked around the room.

"Would you attend that?" he asked with a smirk. I shrugged.

"Maybe. It depends," I said.

"Depends on what?" He took a step closer. An excitement grew in my chest.

"Depends on if I was single or not," I said, looking him square in the eye. He smiled and was about to say something when the announcer came over the speaker, catching me by surprise. For a moment, it felt like it was only us in the room.

"Welcome to the greatest event of Maple Haven's Pumpkin Stampede—the Cowboy Bachelor Auction!" Clapping, hollering and some ear-piercing whistles ensued.

"That's my cue. Will I see you later?" he asked.

"Oh, umm, sure," I said. What I wanted to say was no, because I didn't think I wanted to watch someone else *purchase* a date with him. He smiled and tipped his hat, turning on the heel of his boots and briskly walking away. A woman with a clipboard was walking in my direction, as I assumed she was about to hit the lights.

"Excuse me, are you the gal in charge?" I asked her, with an extra special idea in mind.

"Yes, can I help you?" she asked, giving me a confused look.

"You see those men over there?" I pointed to Tucker's handsome friends. All of them looked very *cowboy* and capable of being a contender for an event based on looks.

"Oh boy. Yes, I do. What about them?"

"I am under the impression that they might want to be a part of this event."

"Really? Are you sure? Geez. The food pantry might be getting a big grant after tonight!" The woman and I chatted for a few minutes, and she left, smiling ear to ear.

I quickly took my seat and got ready to enjoy the show. The lights in the complex went off, leaving a veil of darkness around all of us until our eyes adjusted. All I could see around me was the glow of cell phones held by those waiting to record the show. Then, the stage lit up in a glorious, fantastic manner.

First up was a ranch hand named Miller. He was adorable, probably 19 years old. The announcer said he enjoyed horseback riding, chopping wood, and playing football. He had wavy, brown hair and alabaster skin. I imagined he was what Blair and Cody's adult child would look like, and I smiled at the thought. My eyes widened as he went for a whopping $450 by a girl about his same age. Cute.

Next to the stage was one of Tucker's friends. They introduced him as Ford Donahue. "Ford says his ideal date is flying his lady out to watch him at the NFR," the announcer said, and the crowd was heard getting amped up. Those weren't just any cowboys; those were *rodeo* cowboys. And to the women in our town? That made all the difference. Ford was handsome, but I was taken aback when his total went up to $1,100.

After the rest of Tucker's friends were auctioned off, all but one, that is, as he remained by the refreshments table—I noticed a wedding ring on his finger—I was overjoyed that the amounts were all over $1,000. That might have been the most successful bachelor auction our town had ever put on. I expected Tucker to be next, but the announcer threw a curve ball.

"Up next—ladies, get ready for personal trainer extraordinaire, Dallas Reed!" My jaw dropped. What was Dallas doing at a *cowboy* auction? There was nothing western about that guy, except for the fact that he lived there, but that only made him *western adjacent!* But according to the cheers, the crowd didn't care. Women were standing up and clapping for him as he took the stage. He was wearing jeans for it, which was the first time I'd seen him in anything other than workout clothes, and I didn't love it. It looked weird to me. I laughed at the idea that I had such a crush on that guy whom I'd never even seen in a pair of jeans. Who would've known that would be the straw that broke the camel's back—a pair of Levi's? "Dallas says his perfect date is going for a jog on the beach." I scoffed at that one, too. We didn't even have a beach in Maple Haven! As he stood and spun around, the women around me were lapping it up. He went for an impressive $1,500. The crowd was getting more amped up and the bids were astronomical. Who were these women?

"Next up, is a cowboy you all know and love for his special drinks in their pink cups... Ladies, that's right—we have Tucker Callahan about to take the stage!!!" My heart shattered as the women around me screamed and cheered. Tucker came out, shyly, and gave a little wave to the crowd, unlike all of the other men who strutted like peacocks. I couldn't do that after all. I got up and left, hearing numbers being thrown out in the nine-hundred range before I even got to the door.

Walking to the car, tears welled in my eyes. Why had I done that to myself? I liked Tucker. I realized I'd always liked Tucker but was too blinded by my own stupidity with Dallas to see it. But it was over. I blew it. He was getting auctioned off to be bought up by some gorgeous woman who saw his worth a heck of a lot sooner than I did, and they were going to live happily ever after.

"Ginger?" As I was walking up to my car at the nail salon, Laney called out. "What are you doing here?"

"There was no parking at the county complex, and this is the closest I could get," I laughed, rolling my eyes. "The cowboy bachelor auction is just *that* well attended this year." Laney nodded.

"I heard it went a little viral online a few days ago, and that women were saying they were driving up to twelve hours for a chance to meet a 'real' man." Laney's use of air quotes always made me laugh, because instead of scrunching her fingers, she just waved them in the air like two peace signs.

"Is that so?" I said, looking down at the ground.

"Don't worry, Ginger. I've seen how Tucker looks at you. And how he talks about you. How he *thinks* about you—that day he brought the flowers? He didn't have to do any of that. But he did. Just have a little faith that God will work things out the way they should be. Okay?" Laney was right, per usual, but my feelings were clouding my judgment.

"And what if I don't end up with Tucker?" My voice cracked.

"Then that means God has something even better for you in the future." Laney looked into the salon, where she was standing with the door propped open, and shut it behind her. "Bruce is in there finally changing all those lightbulbs to make them brighter." She lowered her voice. "When I met Bruce, I thought he was just the cutest thing ever of course. Did I show all sorts of crazy right off the bat? In epic amounts," Laney winked. "And did it affect our relationship whatsoever? Also, yes. But for the better. He knew who I was. There was no question I can be a little dramatic sometimes. It was the fast-track of getting to know each other and now we are happily married, and he's here on the most festive week of the year changing lightbulbs. He would do anything for me." As happy as I was for Laney, I failed to get the point she was trying to make.

"What does this have to do with me, Laney? Tucker and I aren't on the same level as you and Bruce. From what I've learned about him, he's learned I have poor judgment for liking Dallas, can't ride a horse to save my life, and I'm pretty self-absorbed. He is the opposite of that." I sighed, taking it all in. "Really, what I like about him so much is his soul. The kindness that he exudes everywhere he goes. And I can't believe I didn't see it sooner."

"That is what I'm saying, Ginger. Tucker is a real man, like Bruce. If it's meant to be with him, none of your origin story will have mattered. The fact is, God still planted him right here in our town. From where you sat inside the salon, you two were facing each other. That's pretty remarkable. Never mind that he needed help and you were confused. Okay?"

"Thanks, Laney." I hugged her, and the moment she gave me a squeeze, her phone chimed. Pulling it out of her back pocket, her blue eyes widened and looked like they might pop out of her head. "What is it?" I asked.

"It's a news alert from that neighborhood group we're in for downtown businesses. The auction just set a record for the amount paid for a bachelor." My heart sank. Truthfully, I wasn't surprised.

"Dang. How much was it?"

"Five thousand dollars!" Laney could barely speak with her jaw dropped as far as it was, and mine was quick to follow.

"Who in the world was the winner? What else does it say?" I wondered if Samantha, with her fancy real estate job and old money swooped in to snag him. Laney studied the post.

"It doesn't say who, but it says it was someone bidding *over the phone.*"

"What is this, a Sotheby's auction? Who calls in over the phone?" Laney and I were both without words.

Favorite Fall Recipes (when appetite is lost)

A freshly-picked apple from a local orchard

2 tablespoons of caramel for dipping

A glass of skim milk

As appetite returns, finish off with an entire store-bought pie (any variety will do)

1 scoop lite vanilla ice cream

CHAPTER 9:
A SEASON FOR SECOND CHANCES

Dressing for a rodeo is like choosing your Sunday best that involves sequins, fringes, lace, and leathers of all kinds. And unlike Sunday, you wear more glam makeup, bigger hair, longer nails—everything is exaggerated. And that's the best part about rodeos: Spectators get to partake in the fun.

My thoughts were a mess as I slipped into my favorite pair of jeans that had jewels all over the back flap pockets, in the shape of horseshoes. I opted for a white tank top with a soft, suede fringe jacket in a beautiful, creamy brown—that particular shade went really well with my red hair. My white, felt cowboy hat and white boots were the perfect touch to the look. And topping it off with copious amounts of bling via my favorite pair of "door knocker" squash blossom earrings with crystal inlay, I was ready to go.

Every year since I was twelve, I sat with Laney and Blair's family in their box seats. Their dad was on the rodeo board of directors, but he never once used his seat, and it was the long-standing tradition that I sit there while he sat with the announcer in the high booth above the grandstand. So, Laney and Blair's mom made it a girl's night whenever we would attend the Pumpkin Stampede-—no men allowed in our box, which I thought worked out fine in the present year, as it would keep Blair's mind off of Cody's absence.

Walking through the gates of the rodeo, I paid the fee to get in. The fringe from my jacket was floating around delicately, tapping me with every step I took. My nerves were almost debilitating as I searched the crowds for Tucker. I just *knew* in my heart he would be there, *once a rodeo cowboy, always a rodeo cowboy.* I went to the box seats and waited for the rest of the ladies to arrive. I saw Laney from a distance wearing her favorite, bright pink cowboy hat and matching pink purse, her smile, the only thing brighter than that combination. As I scoped out the people around me, my eyes darted to a familiar voice coming from the other side of the grandstand.

There he was: Tucker, in the same clothes he wore to the cowboy bachelor auction, helping the junior rodeo kids with their skills. I could only hear syllables and not full words from him, as the voices around me grew louder. As he guided one of the children with roping, I felt my legs stand up and walk towards him like we were two ends of a magnet.

"I didn't think I'd ever see you here," I smiled, knowing full well I hoped on my very last eyelash he would be. Tucker looked up at me in surprise. He was standing in the seating, in a big patch of dirt, helping the kids with their roping before they went on in the pre-rodeo show. I felt like a giant as I looked down at him.

"Well, hello there," he let out a low whistle. "You are looking extra gorgeous tonight, darlin'." Something about his drawl made everything right in the world.

"Thank you," I whispered. I wondered if this was just him being a gentleman, or if he was flirting with me? "So," I took a few steps down towards him so we were standing eye to eye. "Are you going to the hoedown after this? I mean, I know it sounds lame, but I heard this year, there's going to be a disco ball."

"Is that so?" he asked with a laugh, his eyes returning to the kids. "Nah, I don't think so." The disappointment from me was palpable.

"Ah. I suppose you're going out with your auction winner?" I regretted the tone I used immediately. It sounded... Insecure. Upset. *Jealous.* I felt my mouth turn to a frown, and before he could answer, one of the kids needed his help.

"Tucker? Did you see that? I can't do it," the little boy, dressed in head-to-toe denim and a tan cowboy hat, said.

"You absolutely can do it, Wyatt. That's why you're here." Tucker kneeled when he spoke to him. "Here, buddy. Do it like this instead." Tucker took the rope and held it in his hands, and as he waved it, a perfect loop formed at the bottom. "Then, you catch the steer like this!" He roped the steer dummy in one fluid motion. I was impressed but also warmed by his interaction with the little boy. Tucker had so many qualities that I wished I'd seen when I met him.

The little boy, Wyatt, took the rope and did it just like Tucker did, and we all clapped. I felt tears forming in my eyes as Tucker gave him a high five and left him with the confidence to do it again and again. Wyatt kept roping successfully as I stood and lingered another few minutes.

"Well, I'll leave you to it, then," I said with a smile. "Have a good night, Tucker. I'll see you around?" I knew that he might be leaving since the Pumpkin Stampede was over; with winter coming up next, he might be returning home.

"I'm not going on any dates," Tucker called out to me, and I stopped in my tracks, turning around to look at him. "Just for the record. My 'winner' if you will, just did it for charity and does not want a date with me." A feeling of victory took over in my heart. Out of all of the women that bought dates at that auction, year after year, it was the first I'd ever heard of something like that happening.

"*Praise You, Lord!*" I said under my breath, as I could already feel Him working to fix my broken path, just by that simple thing to start.

"What was that?" Tucker asked.

"Praise the Lord," I said, pointing up to God. "What a great thing for that person to do. A lot of people are going to be helped, and I heard it was a record number you got." Tucker nodded.

"Yeah, I guess it was. There's a little more to the story, actually, but these kids need a little more warming up before they take their ponies out and rope."

"Of course. Don't worry about it. It was nice seeing you." I turned and walked back to my seat, taking all the willpower, I had not to turn and look back at him. My heart felt like it was mourning something it never had as I reached my seat.

Laney, Blair, and their mother Kimberly were waiting for me when I got back to the seat. "Hi, Ginger." Kimberly gave me a warm hug, and we all shared platitudes for how everyone was dressed in their full western regalia, per usual. Kimberly returned to having an in-depth conversation with the woman sitting next to her. Blair was a little glum, but Laney had brought a jumbo plastic baggy full of assorted gummy candy, and when she pulled it out of her purse, Blair's eyes brightened up.

"There's my girl," Laney laughed as Blair reached in for a big handful. Once Blair had a mouthful of cinnamon bears, her favorite, Laney's attention turned to me. "So, Ginger." Her lips pursed in a devious smile. "I see Tucker over there..." I finally gave in and turned back to look in his direction. He was standing alone then, overseeing the kids getting lined up for their appearance in the dirt arena.

"Yeah. I asked him if he was going to the hoedown after this." I let out a huge sigh. "He's not." I put my head in my hands. The extra-long fringe on the arms of my jacket spilled all over my jeans.

"What else could one possibly be doing the last night of the Pumpkin Stampede, if not going to the hoedown?" Laney asked rhetorically.

"That's what I thought. So, I asked him if it had anything to do with his *date.* You know, the winner from the auction." Blair and Laney had started chewing the candy furiously, hanging on to my every word as I spoke.

"And!? What did he say?" Laney demanded.

"He said that the *winner* did it purely for charity. And that they did not want a date with him." My voice was down to a whisper as I shared what felt like top-secret information.

"Get out!" Laney stomped both of her boots on the ground, candy spilling from her baggy. I couldn't help but laugh.

"That's just what he said," I shrugged. Laney, standing, looking up-to-no-good, set her bag down.

"I'm going to go take a stroll. Does anyone want anything? Popcorn? Soda? More of the story?" Her tone changed back to a slickly-sweet kindness. Kimberly's ears perked up at that and asked for popcorn.

"Laney! What are you going to do?" I pulled on her sequin sweater. "You're not going over there to talk to him, are you?" My cheeks were reddening as my pulse tripled in speed. Sure, Tucker and Laney had spoken dozens of times. But things had become different. The stakes felt higher. Because they were.

"Who said anything about talking to Tucker? I certainly didn't," Laney put her hand on her chest in protest. "All this candy? A girl needs a little water is all. But if I happen to pass Tucker when I walk out of my way, in the wrong direction, to get to said water—that's a whole 'nother story, my dear."

There were few things in life I understood more than the woman who stood before me in her over-the-top outfit. And I knew that at that time, besides a meteor crashing down into the grandstand and tearing it in half, there was nothing that could stop her from doing whatever it was she was going to do. But with that, she had never been wrong about anything or acted outside of my best interest. So, with a sigh, I pulled out a ten-dollar bill from my pocket and asked for water and a diet soda. Laney, taking the cash, nodded and pranced away, heading straight for Tucker, and I grabbed a handful of candy and ate at it, nervously.

*****

The junior rodeo games were well into play when Laney returned, an eternity later, empty handed, but with a big smile.

"Where's the water? Soda? The popcorn your mom wanted!?" I questioned her and she laughed.

"I'm sorry, it completely slipped my mind. I got caught up in a very *interesting* conversation and lost track of time." She squinted her eyes and smiled.

"What do you mean, interesting?" I bore into her eyes and waited for an answer, but instead, she took another bite of a peach ring and shrugged.

"Oh, I don't know. Maybe on second thought, it's not." I put my hands on her shoulders and squeezed.

"Laney, please tell me! My heart is at stake here." My chin trembled the slightest bit—more from my own candy induced dehydration than anything, but Laney took the bait.

"I can't say anything. I'm sworn to secrecy." She looked at me with a grin. "But, this won't be the last we see of Tucker." My heart skipped a beat.

"He's staying in Maple Haven?" I nearly yelled my question while the rodeo announcer was blasting his introductions as the music cranked up. But when she replied, the music was so blaring along with the cheers from those around us, I couldn't hear her answer. Whatever it was, she was happy about it.

*****

Every year that I was at the Pumpkin Stampede rodeo, I watched the barrel racers in awe: Their long, beautiful curls swaying in the wind as their sequin fringe chaps and jackets dazzled; their powerful horses turning sharply around each barrel. That sport took guts and grit that I would never have, and I appreciated the talent immensely. I watched as a handful of women I knew were participating in that year's competition, taking mental notes so I could congratulate them on their techniques. Finally, my favorite barrel racer and client, Sadie, was up. Having just done her nails, I knew how prepared she was for the competition.

The chute opened, and her horse bolted towards the center barrel. Sadie, bouncing slightly with each gallop, had her hands on the reins and her feet—donned by glitter cowboy boots that I needed to ask her where she got them—were urging the horse to go faster. She looked incredible and noticeably faster than the previous riders. By the time she took the last barrel by storm, her time was several seconds faster than the rest, and she won the competition.

Ginger's Polished Thoughts

I'm not saying Sadie's fresh nail set helped her win. But those glittery nails that dazzled under the romantic rodeo lights didn't hurt nothin', either.

All of our voices were raw at the end of the event from cheering on the contestants; many of them Maple Haven's own. Between the cheers and my silent conversation with God about giving Him the reins of the relationship instead of my self-centered ways I was used to, I felt better about everything by the end.

Hugging everyone goodbye, Laney and Blair explained they were skipping the night's hoedown in lieu of setting up Blair's new home.

"Oh, well, I would rather help too, then. I have no reason to be at the hoedown anyway!" I surmised.

"No!" Laney ordered. "I mean, we got it handled. Just go do your thing and have *fun*, okay?" I shrugged it off but felt that it was suspicious. Thinking it might have to do with her conversation with Tucker, I started to press the topic, but Laney interrupted. "Well, we better get going. Toodaloo!" She wrapped her arm around Blair and briskly walked her to the parking lot.

Toodaloo? I smirked. Checking my watch, the hoedown started only twenty minutes after the last bull rider at the rodeo, which meant I would be there just in time if I got to my car right away. Or... I could stop and get a bite to eat that didn't have sugar in it and still be there with plenty of time for the dance.

Choosing the latter, I drove downtown to get a bowl of soup at the *Buckin' Bronco Bar.* It was an infamous place in town, built and owned by the first Maple Haven rodeo champion who won a world championship at the NFR. It seemed I wasn't the only one with that brilliant idea, because when I walked in, the place was packed. The hostess led me to an open barstool at the bar, gave me a menu, and said the bartender would be with me shortly.

When he finally made his way over to me, his eyes widened. "Hey there. I'm sorry to keep such a beautiful woman waiting." I smiled as he clearly flirted with all the ladies in the place as a part of his job. His wedding ring also told another story. He put his pen to its pad and was ready to take my order. "What can I get you?"

"I'll take a bowl of the spiced chili with a side of the honey corn bread, please." He jotted that down and asked me about a drink. "Got any apple cider tonight? I'm feeling especially nostalgic." He nodded.

"Of course. Only the real, pure pressed apple kind here. One piping hot mug coming right up."

The warmth from the cider warmed my body and soul. When my meal came, I devoured it. Food was such a source of joy for me. I loved indulging in the sweet cornbread with the spicy meats in the chili. It was rejuvenating. Once I paid, I felt myself lingering. The rodeo had been over for almost an hour, though the hoedown didn't end for another three. It was a very long evening—one that I'd never stuck around at past nine and had no intentions of breaking that pattern then. But, slipping my fringe coat back over my arms and washing down the last bit of my cider—that I questioned if it really was freshly pressed since I was gulping grains from the bottom of the cup—I signed the check and left.

If you've ever attended a school dance without a date, then you know what being a wallflower feels like. Not only was there not a single haybale to sit on—all of them already taken by happy couples, groups of friends, or the grandparents of the group who were chaperoning their teenage grandchildren—I was forced by my decision of not arriving early to stand, look, and *feel* even more awkward than I had thought possible.

Disappointedly, Tucker was nowhere to be seen. He wasn't in attendance. It was apparent that I was reading between the lines when Laney had told me I shouldn't come over and help them at Blair's—once again, my shallow ways just heard what I wanted. I was feeling so tired of my struggle and closed my eyes in a silent prayer.

Lord, how can I ever be in a relationship when I make myself the focus of every situation and outcome, repeatedly? It wouldn't even be fair to date someone else who has feelings of their own.

A wild, rambunctious western song came on and almost everyone took the dance floor, opening quite a lot of hay bales in the process. I took a breath of relief as I was able to make myself look a little less desperate by sitting down and people watching. It was always those moments when I wondered how everyone was such a good dancer? Had I missed that day in school when we were taught the basics of the Two Step? Or like anything that required charisma, had someone attempted to teach me, and I'd had partial amnesia and had turned out worse than before on the subject?

Watching everyone *get down* to the music made me almost relieved that I wasn't dancing. I liked to forget that I had two left feet. It was just so much more fun to romanticize the idea of having a date to the hoedown than actually having to execute a dance worthy of said date. Sighing, I got up. It was time to leave. Tucker wasn't there, and at that time, I wasn't in the right state of mind to entertain meeting anyone else. As I turned to exit, my heart stopped beating. Tucker was walking in from across the room, looking in every direction. Could he have been looking for me? Or someone else? After all, he had met nearly every woman in that town, working his truck. The doubts flew through my head. I had been so unabashedly interested in someone else while Tucker and I were hanging out. It was all for his image. He had a whole, big, interesting life outside of my own thoughts. But when he finally locked eyes on me, all of those fears were washed away like water.

I took a step towards him, and he did the same. My steps turned into a walk. The hoedown was in the largest spot we had in the county—there was some ground to cover, and it was amazing that in the dim lighting of that barn-like interior, we could see each other at all. I couldn't take my eyes off of him as we walked toward one another. At one point, I nearly tripped on someone's foot as they were dancing, but I was able to catch myself without breaking his gaze. His mouth turned upward in a handsome smile, with his dimples telling me all was well in the world.

"You're late," I said, when I finally reached him. The yearning between us was electric. I wanted to reach out and put my hands up around his broad shoulders and pull him in for a kiss. I wanted to tell him that I broke the only concrete rule in the pact, other than lying to everyone we know about being in a relationship—*No falling in love?* I might not have been completely to the "L" word, but I was falling faster than a steer at a cattle branding. My heart was head-over-heels for that man, but I felt fantastic and deathly afraid at the same time. What if he pushed me away? Told me I didn't follow the rules? The golden rule? The ONLY rule? My hands were sweating as I wiped them on my jeans, and I felt a moistness appear on my upper lip and hairline. *Ugh.* It was not the day to wear liquid foundation! I took a deep breath and waited for him to respond.

"Sorry. I won't let it happen again," he said as he took a step closer. The intensity between us thickened.

"Can I have this dance?" He held out his hand as the music slowed to a love ballad. I put my hand in his; he immediately spun me around.

"Oh, you're a real dancer, huh?" I put my arms around his neck, and we swayed to the song.

"Had an interesting conversation with Laney at the rodeo," he said.

"So, I should be the one apologizing for *that,*" I smiled. I wanted to come clean about my feelings. I prayed for the right words to say, and as I was waiting for direction, he spoke first.

"It was nothing I wasn't praying for." With his words, it seemed like the room got brighter. My heart was filled with hope. *Thank you, Lord, for making this right.* In my praise, he spoke again. "Ginger, I need to tell you something."

"Anything. Go for it," I said, nervously.

"I wasn't entirely honest with you." My heart sank, and our bodies slowed, releasing our embrace. The options of his confession were endless. Was he dating someone? Was the bidder on the phone wanting more than a date-—he's a male order groom?

"What do you mean?"

"Remember how I said, 'No falling in love'?"

"Yes? What about it?" I stammered. He was calm and collected, while my mind was wringing itself out like a wet towel.

"I said that because I didn't want to mess with what God had in store for us. Truth is, the moment I saw you, I knew you were the one for me." My heart was overflowing with joy as I reached out my hand to take his.

"Tucker, I am so happy to hear that," I beamed. But he didn't return the smile. In fact, he just nodded, and he continued.

"I'm glad, Ginger. But..." Nothing good ever started with that word, "I want to live by God's plan for my life and His timing, and this doesn't seem like the right time."

"Oh." I pulled my hand away in my heartbreaking confusion. "You're *killing* me, Callahan." He said I am the *one* for him... But just *not right now?*

"I just have a few things I need to work on before I can fully commit myself to a relationship," he said. Truthfully, those were words I should've been saying, as I had just been praying about that very thing, but it didn't make it any easier to swallow. *Lord-, please help me out here.*

"As hard as it is to say it, Tucker, I understand that. I've been so self-absorbed the last year—I barely noticed when the right man for me came along at all. So, do what you gotta do. I get it." He reached out and took my hand as I spoke.

"Thank you, Ginger. I know this is crazy... I've found the perfect girl for me—the sassiest redhead in the state of Wyoming—and I'm putting it on pause." he rubbed his forehead in disbelief, "but I've made promises to myself, and God has it in my heart that I want to be the best provider that I can be when it's time to settle down and court my future wife. I don't date just for fun. Never have. I just want you to know I'm serious about you, and I want to get to know everything about you that makes you the way you are, and I can't wait to do it. I just need a few things, including a real place of my own to lay my head at night. I need to be able to offer more than a slice of pie." He leaned in and kissed me softly on the cheek, quickly removing his hat to do so beforehand. His lips sent a shockwave down my spine.

"Walk me to my car?" I asked, revealing a sadness in my voice.

"Of course, darlin'." He took me by the hand, and we walked out of the hoedown. Getting to my car, I leaned up against it. There was still a soft glow of daylight kissing the valleys around us. The streetlights would come on any second. "I promise you that I will call you soon. And when I do, I'd love to take you out on a real, bona fide date that has nothing to do with pumpkin pie."

"Or, horses," I cringed, still shaking off the memory of getting tossed. He laughed.

"I can still smell pine needles in your hair," he leaned in and took in a deep breath of my locks, which I knew smelled like my coconut shampoo, not the great outdoors.

"Yeah, yeah. Okay, then." He was lingering as we spoke. It felt nice to chat. "Hey, you never told me the rest of the story about your caller at the auction?" Tucker nodded.

"Remember, I told you about the rodeo stock contractor's wife who came on to me?"

"Yes. And you turned her down, and they shut you out." The story made me sad.

"Well... You're never going to believe who the caller was," Tucker smiled.

"That woman? Why are you smiling? She sounds like a dangerous person," I hollered, feeling like I needed to defend him.

"Not anymore, it seems." He shrugged. "Turns out, she's become a born-again Christian. Gave up alcohol *and* adultery. She left her number for me to call afterwards and explained the whole thing. I got a very real, humble apology, and the food bank here is getting an extra big grant. Win-win, if you ask me." My jaw dropped.

"That's so great, Tucker. Wow. God really does perform miracles. So, what's next for you, then?"

"That was the other thing. She came clean to the Sage Mountain Rodeo Association about the whole thing, and they offered me a headlining spot at their big rodeo next month if I want to go back." I was quickly calculating the drive time between Maple Haven and Sage Mountain, but I came up short. "I told them no thanks. All that rodeo stuff is behind me. I want to stay here, in Maple Haven." For a moment, it was like I could hear angels singing.

"I'm so glad to hear that, Tucker. Not just about Maple Haven. Of course, I want you here... But you are so gifted at baking. It's really inspiring to be around someone who's so good at what they do." For a moment, I thought about kissing him anyway, but I didn't. "Well, I better go. I hope to hear from you soon, Tucker." The longing between us was mutual as I slipped into my car and drove away.

Small Town Wisdom

Knowing when to walk away is just as important with men as it is with that cake on the kitchen counter that you keep skimming pieces off of.

CHAPTER 10:
FALLING HARDER THAN THE LEAVES

"You'll never guess what happened!" Laney burst through the front door of the salon, standing with her arms up in the air. Her pregnancy was becoming more obvious by the second, and I couldn't wait to meet her baby girl.

"What? There's a sale on desserts and pickles at the grocery store?" I lifted my brows at her. Laney's cravings of late had been quite *adventurous*.

"How did you know that?" Her smile turned into a frown as she waddled over to her chair and pulled out a pint of ice cream from her purse, while digging through it. "Oh no! I forgot the spoon!" Any minute, we were about to have tears unless we found Laney a spoon.

"Blair?" I shot a look across the salon as she was just ringing up a client, but I was in the middle of doing a fresh set of acrylics for Hazel Bayberry, Maple Haven's long-time librarian.

"I'll go find one. Be right back, Laney." This pregnancy had been hard on all of us, because Laney's had been more dramatic and emotional than usual, but we only had five more months to go. How bad could it be?

"Now that's a good color," Hazel remarked. "Perfect for my retirement party." She fluttered her fingers. "This shade of teal has always been my favorite." Putting her hand back under the UV light so the color could cure, I asked more about her retirement plans.

"You've always been at the library. It's going to be so strange without you!" I said.

"I know. Won't it be great? I don't know if I'll ever step in another library again. I've already bought an e-reader. Might just get all my books digitally for the rest of my life." Blair came swooping back into the salon, holding up a spoon like it was an Olympic torch. Hazel continued. "As for my plans? I don't know. I'd like to get one of those accounts where you make videos and strangers from all over the world can comment. I have some tap shoes that are just begging me to slip them on again."

"Ahhh," Laney took a bite of her ice cream. "That's so good. This might be the best ice cream I've ever had." I rolled my eyes.

"You said the mint chocolate chip was the best ice cream you've ever had. And the day before that, it was cookie dough. So, which is it?" I gave her a sideways smile.

"One day, Ginger, you will get it. My taste buds are just going crazy! Everything is tasting better by the moment." She kept eating. "You know what could make this better? Cake!" Mmm. There were few combinations more delicious than cake and ice cream. Except maybe pumpkin pie and ice cream. I looked ahead, past Hazel, out the window behind my client as I'd done every working day at the salon since the hoedown. For the last week, Tucker had been shut down, as his permit was only through autumn. Despite knowing that, I was still surprised when I got there last week to see that his truck had been moved. Tucker had done it while I was gone. He had yet to reach out to me formally.

Under any other circumstances or times in my life, that would have been it; I would've written him off completely. But his working on himself had prompted my own reflective journey with Christ to overcome my self-centeredness and selfish desires. While I was still a work in progress, I'd been led by God to put other people before myself. With the changing of the seasons, He had done more than strip the trees bare from their leaves. In my case, He'd transformed by heart. And right then, I was praying for Tucker, for my friends, family, and my future husband. I didn't know what God had in store for me, but I was letting things in my life happen naturally. I was no longer in the headspace to chase the things that weren't right for me, like before.

Once I finished up with Hazel, I wished her well for her party and cleaned up my station as Lexie was my next client. Blair was preparing to leave, since Cody had just told her that he was coming home for five days over Christmas.

"I'm so excited for you, Blair," I said, as she put away the last of her nail tools. She was going to be out of the salon for the next week while she and Cody spent the holiday together.

"Eek! Thank you. I am, too. I love that man so much. The last few months went by at a glacial pace. I wasn't expecting this surprise, but I am so thankful for it." She was beaming ear to ear as she spoke. "He told me I might not recognize him because he's super tan." We all laughed, trying to imagine it. Cody had alabaster skin just like Blair.

"Have a wonderful time together," I said, as I got up to give her a hug.

"I promise I will!" she said. Leaving the salon, she turned and gave us one last wave. Lexie came through the door as she was leaving.

"Aww, how is Blair doing?" Lexie beamed, the diamond ring on her finger blinding us with its sparkle

"Fantastic. Cody surprised her and is coming home for Christmas!" Laney said, finally putting away her ice cream. "Did you and Mark set a date yet?"

"Well. . ." Lexie put her hand over her mouth politely, showing off the ring once more. "We actually eloped!"

"That's the best news, Lexie! Congratulations," I said, giving her a hug. Laney's client, Samantha, came through the front door and took a seat in a pedicure chair. I hadn't seen much of Samantha of late, but she'd moved on from her apparent early interest in Tucker. Last I heard, she was dating Dallas.

"You're next, missy," Lexie said, as she took a seat in my chair, lowering her voice.

"What do you mean?"

"Marriage. I'm sure of it," Lexie looked at me knowingly. She had all the information I had, every last bit, as I recited what Tucker had told me word for word countless times to her over the past year while she tried to decipher it. At that point, I'd stopped worrying about it completely. It wasn't like I'd met anyone else.

"Why do you say that? Tucker still hasn't called," I sighed, pulling out the nail drill as I slowly started to freshen up her near-perfect acrylics.

"*Because Tucker just bought the Pumpkin Perk Cafe.*" My jaw dropped.

"He WHAT?" My voice echoed through the salon. I felt excited, nervous, and faint, all at the same time. "How did you hear that? Why hasn't he told me?" My thoughts went wild as I considered all of the possibilities. Then, my internal hazard light came on. *Take a breath, Ginger. Not everything is about you.* "I'm so happy for him," I said. And I meant it, with all of my heart.

Ginger's Polished Thoughts

Some days call for fresh nails. Other days call for comfort foods. But every day calls for prayer.

"I didn't hear it, Ginger. I *saw* it. The owners were outside of the cafe, wearing tropical shirts and sandals. I thought that was an odd sight for December, and Mark was taking his sweet time across the street at *Cheap Cuts,* so I had time to gawk for a little bit. Heaven knows he still can't get rid of that bowl haircut." She rolled her eyes and laughed. "Anyway, they handed Tucker the keys and shook hands. Of course, this is just what I saw." My eyes were as wide as they could get. My hands were moving at lightning speed. The faster I could finish Lexie's set, the sooner I could go down there and see it for myself.

"If it's true... That would be the perfect fit for him," I said, nodding.

"It really would. And I sure miss having his pumpkin truck open every day. Since his lease on that spot expired, I haven't found anywhere in town that serves something equally delicious *and* aesthetic."

"The struggle is real," I pointed to my traveling coffee mug. "This thing is older than I am. Still gets the job done, I suppose. But I can't make coffee like that guy can," I grimaced, taking a sip of my drip brew.

"Men are supposed to make coffee. It's in the Bible. *Hebrews.* Look it up," Lexie quipped.

"You're so right! Enough about me. Tell me about your elopement." After finishing up her fresh set and speaking of her newlywed bliss, I stood idly for about fifteen seconds before taking my brown suede shearling coat off the coat hanger by the front door.

"I'll be right back," I announced, to which Laney couldn't respond over her client's talking and just gave a nod. Hesitantly, I stepped outside, closing the door behind me. The weather had gotten quite blustery the past few days as Christmas approached, but most of our snow came in early spring.

I took a few steps down the sidewalk toward the Pumpkin Perk Cafe, walking slowly as I tested the traction on my boots. We had gotten a little sprinkling of rain the previous night before it froze, and while it was warming up again, the walks were quite treacherous. Thankfully, most of the businesses had awnings, but there was still a small gap of exposed concrete.

When I was just two doors down from the Pumpkin Perk Cafe, the heavenly smell of Tucker's espresso machine wafted all the way up my senses. Something with apple and cinnamon was being baked to perfection, and my mouth watered at the sweet fragrance. I closed my eyes as I approached, savoring the scent. When I arrived, I had one second to look into the window and saw Tucker filling up a case of baked goods, when my foot hit a patch of black ice and my legs went up in the air in front of me.

Mere moments went by until Tucker was by my side, in the frigid elements, with a look of grave concern. "Ginger? Are you conscious?" He took both of his rugged hands and carefully straightened my neck, taking extra care to move my hair out of the way.

I lifted up my head. "Oh, geez. This gimmick is getting old." I sat up, feeling dizzying awareness that I was finally close, too close, to that man I'd been yearning for since the Pumpkin Stampede. "I'm okay. Just embarrassed."

"Are you sure? Here, let me help you up. Would you like to come inside?" He motioned towards the door of the cafe. I nodded.

Once I wobbled in, my eyes took inventory as everything in the cafe had changed. The photos on the wall, once generic pictures of coffee cups shot with black and white film, had been replaced with pictures of bull riders in action at the Pumpkin Stampede. There was a beautiful new menu, hung from tan barn wood, with a large blackboard inside. The words were written with festive chalk colors; advertising sweet treats and drinks made with eggnog. He had new furniture made of beige leather, and best of all, the coffee syrups were restocked. The dessert case was full. And colorful leaves were adorning the walls in little frames. I looked in awe at all the different shapes, sizes, and colors that Tucker had collected. It was beautiful.

The place felt like it was thriving again. But the sign said closed, and Tucker and I were the only ones there.

"So, it's true? This is your place now?" I asked, taking it all in. He nodded.

"Yes. It's been a long time coming. Samantha and I have been working on a deal with the owners since that night I met you at the Harvest Moon, remember?" I swatted away my jealousy before it even began. *Thank you, Jesus.*

"I remember you meeting with her, yes." *And I remember how jealous I felt.* Tucker motioned for us to take a seat on his couch, and we did. We sat facing each other, on opposite sides of the couch. "When were you going to tell me? I haven't heard from you since that night at the hoedown."

"Honestly, I was about to head your way in about fifteen minutes." He pointed to a bouquet of flowers on the counter. "I was just making my last preparations. And working on my speech."

"A *speech?*" My eyes widened. "Well, by all means—speech away, Tucker." My body felt like it was shaking from adrenaline even though I was sitting still.

"Ginger, ever since I met you, I wanted to be the best man I could be." I held my breath, waiting for the *"but"*. "I wanted to have something to show for myself. I asked myself, 'How can I be the man to get a woman like Ginger'?" I shook my head.

"Tucker—I didn't need all of this. I just want to be with you." My voice sounded as vulnerable as my heart felt.

"Thank you, Ginger. But if I have nothing to show for myself, where would I be right now? My permit expired, my truck is parked down at the grocery store back alley, and if it wasn't for the apartment upstairs of here, I'd be homeless. I needed to do this for *us.* You deserve a man who puts in the effort to be all that he can be. I'm just sorry it took me this long to do it."

"It has been a long few months..." I trailed off, crossing my arms. "But to be open with you, I, too, had some things I needed to work on. And it turns out, this season of waiting has been fruitful for both of us."

"I'd like to hear more about that, if you care to share," he said.

I nodded. "Sure. Well, if you recall when I met you, I was dealing with some feelings surrounding my self-worth and body image. Vanity. Self-absorption. Obsessive eating habits. Naturally, I was interested in the shallowest man I could think of at the same time, which made for a chaotic combination," I sighed. "Your kindness and not-so-subtle comments helped me see this. And God has been freeing me from these things daily. I'm still a work in progress, especially with little feelings of jealousy. But I'm doing much better now as God continues to shape the woman I am meant to be, inside and out." I was proud that I went to the gym in the morning before work 3–4 times a week then, not 6–7. I had much more balanced eating, which did include indulgences here and there. And carbs. Lots of them. I had gained a little weight back, but with less restriction. My body felt more relaxed at night. I was getting better sleep and enjoying time getting to know the Lord on a deeper level, and how He saw me, while not counting every calorie that went into my body. It was balancing life, while focusing on God.

"You are the most beautiful woman I've ever seen. And even more so now. Whatever you are doing. . . It's working." Tucker gazed at me with an intensity that lit my heart on fire. Would it be the time he would finally kiss me? I was *so* ready.

"You're pretty cute, too, cowboy." I inched a little closer on the couch.

"Is that so?" He put his arm around me. Both of us sat still, aware that we were close enough for our lips to touch. Tucker put his hand around my jaw and started turning his head toward mine. I closed my eyes, making a pout with my lips as I tried to control my breathing. The moment I'd been waiting months for had finally—*a knock on the door interrupted.*

"Are you open yet?" The couple outside waved as they held a newspaper over their heads. The rain had picked back up, but we had been too busy to notice.

"I'm sorry, darlin'." He stood, walking to the door and opening it. The door was unlocked, but with the closed sign illuminated, I was guessing they saw us on the couch and thought they would try to come in. "Hey, guys. I have my soft-opening tomorrow. I'd love for you to come back, then?" The joy in his voice was palpable.

"Yes, we'd love to! We are so glad that it's you that got this place. We've been addicted to your pumpkin chai the last few months." The couple thanked him, then Tucker warned them about the slippery walks, and they left.

"I better get some salt for this ice," Tucker said, hands on his waist as he watched them leave. The kiss moment had passed, and I stood.

"I'm really proud of you, Tucker."

"Thank you, darlin'." He walked over to me and reached his hand out, and I put mine in his. And it felt *good.*

"May I take you on a date tomorrow? Say, seven?" I looked outside. It was nearly pitch black out at four in the afternoon.

"Sure. I get off at six. That should give me enough time."

"I mean seven in the *morning.*" He had a devious smile on his lips, giving way to those dimples again.

"What? Why?" Seven is usually when I wake up in the morning. For that, I'd have to set my alarm for an hour earlier.

"Tomorrow is my soft opening. And I'd like to have my secret ingredient right here, by my side, if you'd honor me with your presence."

Arriving at seven in the morning, I stood for a moment, as there was already a long line formed, and people were fawning over the selection of drinks and food. Tucker had been able to keep the employees from the Pumpkin Perk Cafe, and they seemed happier. I watched as Ray excitedly greeted customers with a fully stocked coffee bar and dessert case, when Tucker came out from the kitchen and took my hand. Electricity ran through my body as he led me into the kitchen and immediately handed me a hot drink in the signature pink cup.

"I'm so glad you're here," he said.

"Me, too," I took a sip of my coffee and savored the taste. It was an eggnog latte; perfectly sweetened and very festive. I didn't know if it was the coffee or the fact that I was finally there with him after those long months, but I was bursting with excitement.

"Are you ready for our date?" he asked, letting go of my hand.

"Yes! But I thought, this was it? Just hanging out?" I motioned to the door. "We can't exactly leave your grand opening," I said. He shook his head.

"I'm calling this a soft opening. My grand opening, I'm planning for after the holidays. I want to do one of those balloon arches and have my family come out. So, you'll be meeting all of them," he winked. "And, I have something for our date right here in the kitchen." He led me to the other side of the room where there were rolling pins, pumpkins, and a slew of fresh ingredients laid out, including a fresh root of ginger. "I thought we could make a pie together." He put an apron over my head, reaching around my waist and tying it. When the bow was in place, he lingered in the hugging position.

"Will you just kiss me already?" I asked.

"Only if you will be my girl," his arms were holding me now, and if they hadn't been, I may have gone weak in the knees from the suspense.

"Yes," I stammered.

"I don't date just for the heck of it." His banter was flirtatious. Daring. Agonizing.

"That's what you said."

"So, if we do this, it's with serious intentions of it ending in a holy matrimony." His eyes narrowed as he spoke, smiling.

"My answer hasn't changed."

"It's just that sometimes I overthink things, and—," I put my finger to his gorgeous mouth and nodded.

"If you don't kiss me, I feel like I might faint from the anticipation." Looking deep into my eyes, I knew his soul spoke the language of my own. When he finally leaned in the gap that was between us, Tucker's passionate kiss was worth the wait.

Favorite Fall Recipe (for a season of waiting)
Big heaping faith in Christ
Several parts prayer
Endless hope
Boundless love for all of those around you

Thank you Jesus, for the season of autumn.

ABOUT THE

AUTHOR

Cassandra discovered her passion for writing at the age of seven when she purchased a diary at the Scholastic Book Fair. What began with journal entries about her school and home life later evolved into a collection of poems, short stories, and novels. Her hobbies include skiing, traveling around the Rocky Mountains, and reading. Much of her writing inspiration stems from her love of dogs, her Onondaga heritage, and her Christian faith. Cassandra's favorite genres of books are Christian fiction novels, Thrillers, and anything British.

She is a full-time writer and resides in the mountains of Wyoming with her husband, Chad.

cassandrajoelle.com

OTHER BOOKS BY CASSANDRA

A Weather Girl's Guide to Love: A Thunderously Sweet Christian Romcom

Partly Cloudy, Mostly Complicated. Hailey Sinclair had her life all mapped out- until God changed the forecast. Instead of being an on-air meteorologist for a national network, she's reporting the weather in rural Wyoming. Now she's caught between her college sweetheart, Jett Dawson, and Colt Wilder- the infuriatingly gorgeous and cheerful cameraman who seems determined to break through her stormy exterior. Torn between the future she planned, and the one God might be writing, Hailey must learn to trust His direction- and her heart- even when it leads straight into the eye of the storm.

Genre: Christian Romantic Comedy

A New Leash on Life: A Dog-Mom Rom-Com, Book 1

Get ready for a hilarious Christian romantic comedy as we follow the journey of a thirty-something introverted woman, Katie Fitzgerald, who's longing for a husband. But when she accidentally adopts a dog, she discovers that love comes in unexpected ways, and that God's timing is always perfect.

Genre: Christian Romantic Comedy

Fetching Love: A Dog-Mom Rom-Com, Book 2

Three couples, three journeys, and one hilarious adventure on the unpredictable path to love. Katie and Eli are ready to say "I do," but the days leading up to the wedding are full of surprises- especially when Katie's mom's true crime sleuthing lands her in a pickle. Samantha and Mitchell seem perfect together, but hidden struggles test their relationship. Can they find common ground, or will their opposing desires pull them apart? Carolyn and Micah have found faith and each other, but their surprise romance leads to a sudden, life- altering decision. As these couples follow the Lord, they find joy and laughter along the way.

Genre: Christian Romantic Comedy

The Après-Ski Proposal: A Romcom About Love Off-Piste

She came for a fresh start... Not a fake boyfriend. When Claire Riley gets dumped on the eve of her 30th birthday, she's blindsided. A spur-of-the-moment ski trip seems like the perfect escape, until she runs into her ex... With his new girlfriend. Shocked and desperate for a lifeline, Claire accepts a proposal from a charming stranger to pose as her fake- boyfriend. What begins as a simple act of saving face turns into a journey that reveals a fresh start in life and love—the kind that only God could have planned.

Genre: Christian Romantic Comedy

The Curse of Josephine Bagley

Over the course of a century, three individuals are woven together by a decades-old curse:

William, after surviving an Indian raid on his orphanage due to his facial disfigurement, goes on to live among the tribe. But when misfortune befalls them, he is quickly traded away and faced with a pivotal choice that changes his life forever.

Josephine has faced immense loss. Despite her granddaughter's efforts to help her find solace in faith, she finds she can't let go of the past and falls further into her belief that she's eternally bound to darkness.

Saraphina, a fledgling antiques dealer, gets the surprise of her life when a courier delivers notice that she's the last surviving relative of the Bagley Estate. What seemed like a windfall that could help her career now causes her to question her own reality.

In this tale of intertwining mystery, loss, and faith, these souls navigate through nefarious trials to find the gift of grace and forgiveness that extends to us all.

Genre: Christian Gothic

www.ingramcontent.com/pod-product-compliance
Lightning Source LLC
Chambersburg PA
CBHW032247310726
48973CB00008B/2330

9 798991 048859